"You don't mean that I'm...?"

"Still my wife? That's exactly what I mean."

"No, I *can't* be," Elizabeth cried desperately. "The marriage was going to be annulled."

"That was your idea," Quinn reminded her. "You didn't wait to see if I was in agreement."

"But when I swore I had no intention of living with you, the family lawyers drew up the necessary papers and I signed them."

"Well, I didn't...."

LEE WILKINSON lives with her husband in a three-hundred-year-old stone cottage in a village in Derbyshire, England. Most winters they get cut off by snow! Both enjoy traveling, and previously joined forces with their daughter and son-in-law, spending a year going round the world "on a shoestring" while their son looked after Kelly, their much-loved German shepherd dog. Lee's hobbies are reading and gardening and holding impromptu barbecues for her long-suffering family and friends.

Books by Lee Wilkinson

HARLEQUIN PRESENTS®
1991—A HUSBAND'S REVENGE
1933—THE SECRET MOTHER
2024—WEDDING FEVER

LEE WILKINSON

Marriage on Trial

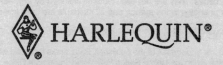

HARLEQUIN®

TORONTO • NEW YORK • LONDON
AMSTERDAM • PARIS • SYDNEY • HAMBURG
STOCKHOLM • ATHENS • TOKYO • MILAN • MADRID
PRAGUE • WARSAW • BUDAPEST • AUCKLAND

ISBN 0-373-12090-7

MARRIAGE ON TRIAL

First North American Publication 2000.

Visit us at www.romance.net

Printed in U.S.A.

CHAPTER ONE

GUESSING that the occasion would be a glittering one, Elizabeth, unable to compete, had chosen simplicity: a midnight-blue cocktail dress, silk-clad legs, plain suede court shoes, and her long, sable-dark hair in an elegant chignon.

Her fingers were ringless, and she wore no jewellery apart from a watch on her left wrist and earrings in her neat lobes. Made of silver and mother-of-pearl, intricately curved in the shape of a mermaid, they were extremely old and very beautiful.

She was ready and waiting when the bell rang.

Slipping into her grey, fun-fur coat and picking up her squashy bag, she opened the door of her tiny mews cottage and smiled at the tall, well-built man wearing impeccable evening clothes.

Richard Beaumont bent his head and kissed her cheek. 'You look delightful, as always.' His voice was clear and cultured, his blond hair brushed smooth, his aristocratic face full of charm.

The November evening was dark and damp, with more than a hint of fog in the air. By the black-painted door of Cantle Cottage a yellow rose, still flowering bravely, was beaded with moisture, and in the light shed by the old-fashioned street lamps the wet cobbles gleamed like golden fish scales.

'What time does the sale start?' Elizabeth asked, as he helped her into the Beaumonts' chauffeur-driven limousine.

'Nine-thirty, after a champagne buffet. Because it's a small, private collection of gems that are being sold, the auction itself should be over fairly quickly.'

Wealthy, and a lover of beautiful things, Richard collected precious stones as another man might collect postage stamps.

'Will you be bidding for anything special?' she asked, as the sleek car pulled out of the cul-de-sac hidden away in the heart of town, and turned towards Hyde Park.

His blue eyes shone with enthusiasm. 'Very special. The Van Hamel diamond.'

'Is there likely to be much competition?'

'Though only a relatively small, select group of people have been invited, I'd be surprised if there wasn't quite a lot.'

'But you will get it?'

Smiling at the thought of being beaten, he answered with supreme confidence, 'Oh, yes, I'll get it. It's not particularly large, but it's flawless, and the cutting is exquisite. It would make a perfect engagement ring.'

This last was added so casually that she blinked.

'You seem surprised.'

She had guessed that he was getting serious, but unsure of herself, of what she wanted, she hadn't known whether to be pleased or anxious.

Neither an impetuous youth nor a man to mistime things, apparently reading her indecision, Richard had played a waiting game, asking for nothing more than her company, refusing to press her.

Until now.

They were held up by traffic signals, and in the light from the street lamps he studied her half-averted face, the sweep of dark lashes, the straight nose, the warm curve of her lips, the pure line of her jaw. 'Surely you know I love you and want to marry you?'

Though aware that he was expecting some response to his declaration, thrown by the suddenness of it, she remained silent while her thoughts whirled.

The only son of a baronet, he was a handsome, charismatic man, polished and considerate. A brilliant brain and an unsurpassed knowledge of the world's stock markets had made him wealthy in his own right, and well respected in business circles.

She was twenty-six. If she wasted this chance, there would be very few other men to come anywhere near him, and she wanted a real home and children while she was still young.

After a moment, his voice even, he added, 'If the answer's yes, I thought after the auction we might go back to my apartment?'

As well as the Beaumonts' large Georgian house in Lombard Square, which Elizabeth knew well, Richard had a suite of rooms at a Park Lane hotel, which she didn't know at all.

Conventional in many ways, he was making it abundantly clear that, though he'd accepted a more or less platonic relationship so far, he wasn't prepared to keep on doing so.

It was make-your-mind-up time.

So what was she to do? It was more than five years since her life had fallen apart. She was genuinely fond of Richard, so surely it should be possible to put the past behind her and start living again? To give him the commitment he was asking for?

'Well, my dear?' he pressed.

She turned to look at him, her clear, dark grey eyes steady. 'Yes, I'd like that.'

With a little smile of triumph, he took her hand and squeezed it. As they moved off once more, he said, 'I don't see any need for a long engagement, so will you give some thought to a spring wedding...?'

A moment later they were leaving the main road and

turning into Belham Place. Belham House, where the sale was being held, was a blaze of lights.

Originally a small palace, the beautiful old building was set back behind a grey stone wall surmounted by black and gold spiked railings.

A uniformed policeman was standing by the tall, ornamental, wrought-iron gates. After a glance at Richard's gilt-edged invitation card, he waved them through.

The chauffeur drove past an apron crowded with cars and set them down by an imposing, studded door guarded by a plain-clothes officer.

'You needn't wait, Smithers,' Richard informed his driver crisply. 'We'll get a taxi back.'

Elizabeth gave him full marks for discretion.

Once inside the marble-floored and pillared foyer her coat was whisked away by a liveried attendant. A moment or two later they were being greeted by their silver-haired host—an impoverished earl, she learnt later—before being handed a glass of vintage champagne.

When they joined the other well-dressed guests in the chandelier-lit dining hall, Richard introduced her to several of his acquaintances, then, *sotto voce*, pointed out a couple of security men mingling inconspicuously with the crowd.

During an excellent buffet, where the champagne flowed freely, her companion appeared to be his usual cool, relaxed self, but she could sense a simmering excitement, a feeling of expectancy beneath the surface calm.

As nine-thirty approached, the assembled company moved through to the salesroom: a large salon, with double doors at each end. At the entrance they were each presented with a catalogue, before being shown to their seats.

A slim, sprightly man with fair, thinning hair carefully styled to hide incipient baldness, took his place on the auctioneer's stand. He tapped with his gavel, and the sale began.

Some exceptional stones, both cut and uncut, came up but, his face impassive, Richard showed no particular interest until the last item was reached.

Clearing his throat, the auctioneer announced, 'The final lot is a diamond of the first water, known as the Van Hamel...'

He went on to give precise details of its provenance, before suggesting, 'May I start the ball rolling at two hundred and fifty thousand pounds?'

The bidding moved cautiously, as would-be buyers tried to judge the extent of the opposition. Richard watched and waited, his hands lying lightly in his lap, making no move.

Only when the price had reached three hundred and fifty thousand did he join the fray with a flick of his catalogue.

Two of the other bidders dropped out fairly quickly, making it a straight fight between Richard and a middle-aged, genteel-looking lady, whom earlier he'd identified as a dealer.

A ruby flashing fire whenever she raised her hand, she hung on tenaciously, and the price had been pushed up another fifty thousand before she shook her head, signalling defeat.

'Four hundred thousand pounds,' the auctioneer repeated for the third time, and raised his gavel.

Richard gave a murmur of satisfaction and smiled at Elizabeth, who smiled back.

But, his gaze travelling to the rear of the room, the auctioneer paused. Having lifted his brows questioningly, he nodded and announced, 'Four hundred and fifty thousand pounds.'

A murmur of excitement rippled through the audience like a breeze through a cornfield.

Up till now, bidders had been raising the price by five or ten thousand pounds a time. The newcomer had raised it by fifty thousand in a single bid.

It was tactics, meant to be the *coup de grâce*, she realized dazedly.

Momentarily, Richard looked staggered, then, his blue eyes gleaming with the light of battle, he coolly topped the previous bid by the same amount.

Impassively, the auctioneer repeated the latest figure and looked across at the other contender, who responded promptly.

Elizabeth bit her lip. She'd been hoping that dramatic first bid was the only shot in the newcomer's armoury. Clearly it wasn't.

Raising it another fifty thousand, Richard asked in an undertone, 'Can you see who's bidding against me?'

She turned to peer cautiously over her shoulder, and saw a man wearing immaculate evening dress lounging nonchalantly against the far wall. He was looking away from her, but the arrogant set of that dark head, the easy stance were only too familiar.

The breath caught in her throat and her heart seemed to stop. No, no, it couldn't be Quinn. It *couldn't*.

He moved slightly, giving her a clear view of his hawk-like profile.

Oh, dear God, it was! There was no mistaking that powerful, hard-boned face... She felt faint and dizzy, as if all the blood was draining from her body.

While shock kept her eyes fixed on him, he raised the bidding once more with a slight movement of his index finger.

Until then she hadn't considered the possibility that Richard might lose. Now she realized it was a battle of the giants.

Terrified that if she kept on looking Quinn might notice her, she dragged her gaze away and turned to the front.

Richard gave her a questioning glance.

Her mouth desert-dry, she shook her head.

Another flick of his catalogue and he was momentarily on top, the bidding running now at seven hundred thousand.

There was a slight pause, and Elizabeth felt a stir of hope. Then the auctioneer was announcing, 'Eight hundred thousand pounds.'

A rise of one hundred thousand pounds.

The audience gasped.

Richard's jaw tightened, and with an abrupt movement he indicated that his part in the proceedings had ended.

Elizabeth, shaken to the core, was bitterly sorry for him. She guessed that, though he would probably have given even more for the diamond, in the face of such competition he must have thought it lunacy to continue bidding.

The moment the sale was declared over, he rose, and, a hand beneath her elbow, helped her to her feet. Although he was hiding his disappointment and chagrin beneath a spurious air of calm, it was obvious he couldn't wait to get out of the place.

Neither could she.

Quinn mustn't see her. *He mustn't.* She stifled a panicky urge to push her way through the crowd and bolt.

Richard's hand at her waist, a hollow sensation in the pit of her stomach, she started to move towards the nearest exit as fast as the slow-moving throng would allow.

A glimpse of a tall, dark-haired man brought her heart into her mouth, but a second look showed he was at least forty, with a beefy face and a paunch.

They had reached the doors when one of Richard's acquaintances drew level. 'Hard luck,' he remarked sympathetically. 'But what can you do against opposition like that?'

'Did you see who it was?'

'Yes, it was Quinn Durville, a multimillionaire banker from the States. I heard a whisper that he came over specially, so he must have intended to get it.'

'I should have known,' Richard said morosely as the other man moved away. 'I've come up against Durville before...'

Elizabeth felt as though she'd been kicked in the solar plexus. She had never dreamt that the two men might have met. It was so *unlikely*. Yet wasn't there an old saying 'The most unlikely thing to happen is nearly always the thing that does happen'?

His face set, Richard was going on, 'When it's something he wants, the swine doesn't give any quarter, and he won't let anything stand in his way.'

It was the simple truth. About six weeks after she'd left him, a man who was obviously a hired detective had tracked her down and started to watch her every move.

Realizing then how utterly ruthless Quinn could be, and knowing she could never go back to him, she had been forced to run, to change her name and find a fresh place to hide.

She shuddered at the memory.

Richard felt the slight movement and, his manner cool and controlled again after that brief, betraying flash of anger, asked, 'You don't know Durville, do you?'

Somehow she found her voice and answered, 'No.'

'Is there something wrong?' Richard sounded solicitous. 'You're looking distinctly pale.'

'I'm fine, really. I expect it's just reaction.'

Coffee was being served in the dining hall. 'Would you like to sit down and have a cup?' he suggested.

'No!' Then, more moderately, she said, 'No, thank you.'

His relief was evident. 'In that case I'll get your coat.'

Though he returned quite quickly with it over his arm, to Elizabeth it seemed a long time before she'd slipped it on and they were making their way across the foyer.

They were nearing the door when a man with crisp, peat-dark hair, easily topping six feet, and looking even bigger because of the breadth of his shoulders, appeared from behind a pillar.

As if he'd been lying in wait to intercept them, he moved purposefully to block their way.

Elizabeth's heart lurched and began to race with suffocating speed. Face to face with this man she had hoped never to see again, she tried to stay calm, to convince herself that no matter what happened he could no longer hurt her.

But she was unable to do either. She felt sick with fear and remembered pain.

Sparing her barely a glance, the newcomer held out his hand to Richard. 'Ah, Beaumont... You put up a good fight.' The words only just escaped being patronizing.

Hiding his antagonism, Richard shook the proffered hand and remarked, 'I fancy this makes us even?'

'I hardly think so,' Quinn disagreed smoothly.

There was a brief pause. When he showed no sign of moving away, impelled by good manners, Richard began the necessary introduction.

'Elizabeth, may I present Mr Quinn Durville...?'

A kind of despairing pride kept her head high while she looked into that lean, autocratic face, with its high-bridged nose and chiselled mouth, and waited for Quinn to say they knew each other very well.

Feeling the tension already crackling between the two men, she was well aware that Richard would find the news unwelcome, to say the least.

It wouldn't have been quite so bad if she'd confessed to knowing Quinn when he'd asked her... But, by denying it, she had effectively involved herself in a deception.

'Durville, my fiancée, Miss Cavendish.'

Quinn took her hand and said a perfunctory, 'I'm pleased to meet you, Miss Cavendish.' His glance was cool and impersonal and, to her amazement, the greeting held nothing but conventional courtesy.

She drew a deep, unsteady breath, hardly daring to believe he hadn't recognized her.

Of course he wouldn't know the name Cavendish, and, having been christened Josian Elizabeth, she had been known from childhood as Jo...

Added to that she had altered a great deal in the time they'd been apart. Then, her fine bones had been smudged beneath a layer of puppy fat, her thick, silky eyebrows unshaped, her hair short and curly.

But perhaps the biggest change lay in her manner. Gone was the curvaceous, casually dressed girl, with a smiling mouth and laughing eyes, who had been as naïve and friendly as a Labrador puppy.

In her place was a slender, elegantly dressed woman, poised and sophisticated, her grey eyes guarded, her mouth vulnerable.

Oh, yes, she'd altered. Enough, it seemed, to save the stress and trauma that would surely have followed if Quinn *had* identified her.

As his warm clasp closed around her cold fingers, she felt her legs start to tremble and every nerve-ending in her body tighten in response to his touch.

He had always possessed a potent physical attraction that had been able to draw her like a magnet and hold her even against her will.

Panic-stricken, she reminded herself that she was a mature woman now, no longer young and susceptible, and no longer on her own. She had Richard. If the need arose, he would be a rock she could cling to.

Though surely it *wouldn't* arise? Judging by Quinn's distant civility, he'd forgotten her entirely, so she was safe, thank God.

Or was she? Could he be playing some deep dark game?

Well, if he was, she had little option but to go along with it.

Somehow, she managed a husky, 'How do you do?' before withdrawing her hand.

'Have you been engaged long, Miss Cavendish?'

The question startled her, and as she gaped at him stupidly Quinn added, 'Only I notice you're not wearing a ring.'

Turning to a thin-lipped Richard, he smiled a shade tauntingly. 'It made me wonder if perhaps you had a special reason for wanting the Van Hamel diamond?'

Quinn had always had a brain as sharp as a razor, she thought with reluctant admiration.

Pointedly ignoring the question, Richard said curtly, 'Will you excuse us?' He took Elizabeth's elbow. 'If we don't get moving we'll have a job to find a taxi.'

Continuing to block their way, Quinn enquired, 'Where are you heading?'

'Park Lane.' Obviously Richard was finding it an effort to remain civil.

'As it happens, I'm going that way myself...'

Sensing what was to come, and desperate to get away, she froze.

'I have a car, so I'll be happy to drop you.'

Tension making her hold her breath, she glanced at Richard's face, and was cheered to see that he was about to refuse.

Before he could speak, however, Quinn went on urbanely, 'If you're still interested in owning the Van Hamel, maybe we could talk about it on the way?'

By her side, Elizabeth felt Richard tense. He badly wanted the diamond. Would he be willing to sink his pride and negotiate?

But why should *Quinn* be disposed to?

If it was true that he'd come over from the States specially to get the Van Hamel, why should he be prepared to part with it to a rival?

There was something disturbing about the offer, something that put her in mind of, '"Will you walk into my parlour?" said the spider to the fly...'

She repressed a shiver, and with every ounce of her concentration willed Richard to reject it.

But, after an endless few seconds, to her consternation, he agreed, 'Very well.'

Her stomach churning, she moved to rejoin the straggle of people still discussing the evening's events.

As they headed for the main exit, she noticed two women pause in their conversation to glance covertly at Quinn. Without being conventionally handsome, he had the kind of tough, dynamic good looks that attracted and held the attention of most females.

Outside the fog had thickened. On the apron, car doors slammed and engines purred into life as they accompanied Quinn to a silver-grey Mercedes parked nearby.

He produced a key and opened the doors. Before Elizabeth could form any kind of protest she found herself being helped into the front passenger seat, while Richard, looking anything but pleased, was forced to climb into the back alone.

A moment later Quinn had slid behind the wheel and was querying, 'Quite comfortable, Miss Cavendish?'

In the light from the dashboard his green eyes met and held hers. Just for an instant she fancied both his question and his glance held derision, as if he was well aware of how very *uncomfortable* she was. But then it was gone, leaving just a polite enquiry from a stranger.

'Yes, thank you,' she answered flatly.

Their headlights like searching antennae in the foggy air, they joined a stream of vehicles following each other through the gates and into Belham Place.

Beyond the quiet square the streets were busy, and as they negotiated the Friday-night traffic Quinn asked, 'What do you do for a living, Miss Cavendish? Or perhaps you don't need to actually work?'

Disliking both the question and the way it had been phrased, she hesitated before responding stiffly, 'I'm Lady Beaumont's secretary.'

'Really? Well, if the position is a live-in one—'

'It isn't,' Richard broke in brusquely. Then, with barely masked annoyance, he said, 'You indicated that you were prepared to talk about the diamond?'

'Ah, yes, the diamond...' Quinn mimicked the other man's cut-glass accent. 'For a stone of its size it aroused a fair bit of interest.'

'I heard you came over specially for the sale?' Apparently Richard also had doubts.

'Did you?' Quinn, it seemed, was giving nothing away. Slipping neatly between a bus and a taxi, he added conversationally, 'In the event, I almost missed it. Due to some last-minute technical fault, our landing was delayed. I only just managed to change, pick up a hire car, and get to Belham House in time.'

If only he *hadn't*, Elizabeth thought with a sigh.

Sounding distinctly sour, Richard remarked, 'I'm surprised you didn't bid by phone.'

A slight smile tugging at his lips, Quinn responded trenchantly, 'Bidding by phone tends to be rather tame, don't you think? I get more of a buzz from actually being there. Especially when there's some action.

'I must admit I was expecting rather more excitement in regard to some of the earlier lots...'

Elizabeth knew well that Quinn wasn't a man for small talk, and, staring straight ahead, listening to his low-pitched, slightly husky voice analyzing the sale, she wondered what he was up to.

It was a little while before it dawned on her that rather than actually getting down to discussing the diamond he was employing delaying tactics.

But why?

When they reached Park Lane, with a glance in the rear-view mirror at his back-seat passenger, he broke off what he was saying to enquire, 'The Linchbeck, isn't it?'

Without waiting for an answer, he turned into the forecourt and drew to a stop outside the entrance to the quiet, exclusive hotel.

Aware that just by knowing the exact address Quinn had gained a subtle advantage, Elizabeth bit her lip as he came round to open her door.

Richard climbed out, and, his face expressing his annoyance, asked shortly, 'Perhaps we could make an appointment to talk about the Van Hamel? Would any particular time and place suit you?'

'There's no time like the present,' Quinn suggested, his voice bland.

Elizabeth felt sure that in the circumstances, and after the evening's debacle, Richard would choose to wait until he'd fully regained his cool.

But to her surprise he agreed. 'Then perhaps you'll join us in the bar for a drink?'

'Your suite would be preferable,' Quinn said smoothly. 'Rather more private.'

So there was the answer to her question, Elizabeth thought uneasily. For some reason of his own, Quinn wanted to see the other man's apartment.

Convinced now that Richard was being *manipulated*, she found herself praying that he would tell his tormentor to go to the devil.

But before he could speak the doorman said a cheerful, 'Nasty evening,' and held open the heavy glass door.

Richard nodded abruptly and, his jaw tight, led the way inside and across the luxuriously carpeted foyer to the lift.

Elizabeth was five foot seven, fairly tall for a woman, but sandwiched between two men who both easily topped six feet she felt dwarfed, loomed over.

When they left the lift at the top floor, she took care to keep Richard between herself and Quinn until they reached the apartment.

The sitting room, with its plum-coloured curtains and carpet, its leather suite and sporting prints, was handsome, comfortable, and undoubtedly masculine.

After slipping her coat from her shoulders and hanging it in a recessed cupboard, Richard moved towards a small but well-stocked bar. 'What would you like to drink, darling?'

She half shook her head. 'I'd prefer a coffee later, thank you.'

Motioning his unwelcome guest to take a seat, Richard picked up the whisky decanter and queried, 'Durville?'

'I'm driving, so I'll stick with coffee.'

Clearly in need of a drink, Richard poured himself a stiff whisky and swallowed a mouthful.

As he turned towards the kitchen, Quinn asked casually, 'Mind if I take a look around? At one time I had a service flat in the Brenton Building, but I gave it up...'

Recalling her own brief stay there, Elizabeth shuddered. What should have been the happiest night of her life had turned into a nightmare.

'Now I'm considering having a *pied-à-terre* here, for the times I'm in London,' Quinn was going on, 'rather than staying at hotels.'

His interest open, undisguised, with cool effrontery he began to prowl, peering first into a small study and then into a good-sized bedroom and bathroom.

Tense and ill at ease, Elizabeth perched on the edge of

a chair and watched him warily. Oh, why had he come back into her life just when she was about to make a new commitment?

She had found it impossible to forget him, but she had almost succeeded in leaving the past behind, in convincing herself he no longer mattered.

But the past had suddenly caught up with her, and he *did* matter. Even though she feared and resented his presence, just the sight of him took her breath away and left her full of the bitter-sweet longing he had always effortlessly aroused in her.

Glancing in her direction, Quinn met her eyes.

Terrified of what he might read in them, she looked hurriedly away. It seemed he had blotted out both her and the past, and the last thing she wanted to do was remind him.

He came and sat down opposite, his ease mocking her lack of it. After a thoughtful scrutiny, one dark brow raised, he observed, 'I take it you don't live here, Miss Cavendish?'

Wanting to consolidate her position as Richard's fiancée, she was loath to admit it. 'What makes you think that?' She strove to sound dismissive, even slightly amused.

'There are no signs of female occupancy, and if you *had* lived here I'm fairly sure *you* would have made the coffee.'

'A male chauvinist, I see,' she said sweetly.

'Not at all.'

'But you consider a woman's place is in the kitchen?'

His smile mocking, he said, 'I can think of a better place for a woman to be.'

Her colour rising, she looked anywhere but at him.

'So where *do* you live, Miss Cavendish?'

Her impulse was to say sharply that it was none of his business. Common sense warning that overreacting might make him suspicious, she stayed purposely vague. 'At the moment I'm living in a small cottage.'

'A mews cottage?' It was as though he could read her mind.

'Yes.'

'In the West End?'

Whatever his motives for wanting to know, it was clear that he wasn't going to be put off.

'Hawks Lane,' she said, hoping against hope that he hadn't the faintest idea where that was. 'If you'll excuse me,' she added coldly, 'I'll see if Richard needs any help.'

At that precise moment their host reappeared, carrying a tray with two cups of coffee.

When they had each been handed a cup, a slightly belligerent look on his face, Richard swallowed the rest of his whisky and, still standing, turned to the other man. 'I was hoping to have an early night, so if we can discuss the diamond without further delay?'

'Of course,' Quinn agreed, his tone equable.

A moment or two passed in silence.

When it became obvious that the ball was in his court, a touch of angry colour appearing along his cheekbones, Richard suggested shortly, 'Perhaps you'll be good enough to name your price?'

'Before I do, I'd like to know why you're so keen to have that particular stone.'

There was another taut silence before, clearly at the end of his patience, Richard admitted, 'You were right earlier. I was hoping to have it set into an engagement ring. If that puts the price up—'

'Just the opposite,' Quinn broke in. 'In fact I'll let you have it for the exact amount I'm paying for it.'

Elizabeth was once again besieged by doubts and misgivings. Why was he willing to part with a diamond he'd taken so much trouble to acquire, without making a profit?

It simply didn't make sense.

CHAPTER TWO

RICHARD said slowly, 'That's very decent of you.' Then, proving he had the same kind of doubts as Elizabeth, he asked, 'May I ask why?'

'Call it a wedding present.' Quinn's smile was sardonic. 'I'll be in touch tomorrow to complete the transaction.'

'I'm in Amsterdam for the weekend. I fly back Monday morning.'

'Say Monday afternoon, then?'

'Fine. I'll be at Lombard Square.'

Quinn put down his untasted coffee and rose to his feet. 'Now, you mentioned that you wanted an early night, so I'll get moving.'

Elizabeth drew a deep breath. He was going, and with a bit of luck she'd never have to see him again.

The evening had been a great strain, but she should be thankful for two things at least: Quinn hadn't recognized her and, for whatever reason, he'd made no attempt to hold Richard to ransom over the diamond.

'Let me see you out.' Failing to hide his relief, Richard turned to lead the way to the door.

Standing where he was, Quinn said, 'I'll be happy to see you home, Miss Cavendish.'

His quiet announcement shook her rigid.

'N-no, really…' she stammered. 'I couldn't put you to so much trouble…'

The very last thing she wanted was for Quinn to see her home. But neither, she suddenly realized, did she want to stay at the apartment.

Since she'd agreed to come back with Richard, the whole

mood of the evening had altered. So much had happened that both her mind and her emotions were in a whirl. She needed time to think, to get over the shock of seeing Quinn again.

As it was, she knew it would be impossible to go to bed with Richard tonight without a dark, mocking face coming between them...

Shuddering at the very idea, she added jerkily, 'I'll get a taxi later.'

She must talk to Richard. Tell him she had a headache... Make some excuse...

'I doubt if there'll be any taxis willing to venture out.' Quinn's level tones penetrated her thoughts. 'The fog's getting thicker by the minute.'

He indicated the windows, where nothing was visible but opaque grey mist. 'If you don't leave with me now, you'll almost certainly be stuck for the night.'

Suppose he was right? If she *was* stuck, with only one bedroom it could prove difficult...

'And believe me it's no trouble,' he added briskly. 'I pass the end of Hawks Lane.'

As though the matter was settled, he strode across to the cupboard, retrieved her coat and held it for her.

Seeing that a furious-looking Richard was about to intervene, Elizabeth made up her mind. Giving him a speaking glance, she said, 'In the circumstances I think it would make sense to go.'

Just for a second he looked ready to protest, then, apparently thinking her decision was because she wanted to observe the proprieties, being a gentleman, he stayed silent.

Slipping into her coat, she went on a shade awkwardly, 'It's been a tiring evening, and I'm more than ready for some sleep.'

If they'd been alone, Richard would almost certainly have taken her in his arms and kissed her with pleasurable skill and expertise, but, clearly inhibited by the other man's presence, he gave her a mere peck on the cheek.

'You're off on Monday, aren't you?' His voice was tightly controlled. 'So I'll see you Tuesday. Perhaps we can go to Swann Neilson and discuss a suitable setting for the diamond?'

'Lovely.' She managed to smile at him, while a strange presentiment made a chill run through her.

'Was that shiver caused by cold or excitement?' Quinn's mocking voice asked, as they left the penthouse together.

Without thinking, she answered, 'Neither. Just a goose walking over my grave.'

His heavy-lidded eyes gleaming green as a cat's between thick dark lashes, he remarked softly, 'I once knew a girl who used to say that.'

Elizabeth cursed her careless tongue as, a hand at her waist, Quinn escorted her across the small foyer and into the lift.

Like some jailer, he stood much too close for comfort, but, afraid to move away in case it was obvious, she made herself stay where she was.

They descended without speaking, while she tried to convince herself that his remark had just been an idle one.

But suppose he'd guessed? Her blood ran cold at the thought.

Oh, why on earth had she left with him? In retrospect it had been a stupid and dangerous thing to do. Like jumping out of the frying-pan into the fire.

At least she would have been *safe* with Richard. If she'd simply told him that she didn't want to sleep with him, he wouldn't have pressed her.

Or would he?

He didn't take kindly to being disappointed, and nothing had gone as he'd planned.

Still, he wasn't an insensitive man, and without knowing

the truth about Quinn surely he would have appreciated that the evening's events had affected her, and forgiven her change of heart?

But now it was too late.

Outside, the fog was dense and clammy, enveloping the hotel entrance, obscuring the ornamental façade and turning the wrought-iron lamps into hovering, luminous ghosts.

There were hardly any pedestrians about, and a lot fewer cars than usual, the normal Park Lane traffic noise muffled and muted.

'Looks pretty bad, sir,' the doorman remarked.

'Conditions certainly aren't improving,' Quinn agreed, dropping a generous tip into his ready palm.

'Perhaps it would be wiser to stay?' Elizabeth suggested eagerly. 'They'd almost certainly have a room, and it would save you having to drive in this.'

'I don't see it as a problem.' Already the car door was open and, a hand beneath her elbow, Quinn was helping her in. 'I've driven in worse.'

As they joined the slow-moving traffic and began to crawl through fog-shrouded streets, tense and nervous, she stared straight ahead, until the amorphous grey mass made her eyes ache.

Needing to break a silence that was lengthening and beginning to get intolerable, she said, 'This is the kind of fog one reads about in Victorian melodramas.'

Her normally clear, well-modulated voice sounded somewhat hoarse and strained.

'Don't tell me you read Victorian melodramas?' While pretending to be shocked, Quinn's sidelong glance was tolerant, even a trifle amused.

Relaxing a little, she admitted a shade ruefully, 'I've developed quite a passion for them.'

He laughed. 'Does Beaumont approve of your taste in literature?'

'I've no idea.'

'You don't appear to know each other too well.'

'We know each other very well.' Even as she spoke she was aware that wasn't the truth. Richard only knew the cool, collected, rather reserved woman she had become.

All her warmth and passion, her easy gaiety and generosity of spirit, her *joie de vivre*, were dead and gone, buried beneath the tombstone of the past.

'When did you two meet?' The question seemed to be an idle one.

'When I started to work for Lady Beaumont.'

'And when was that?'

Elizabeth wondered whether he was genuinely interested or just making polite conversation. But either way it seemed better to talk than sit in silence.

'Last February,' she answered. And, feeling on relatively safe ground, she went on, 'The writer I had been working for was going abroad. I needed to find another job, so I joined an agency who sent me as a temp, after Miss Williams, Lady Beaumont's secretary, went down with flu.

'Then in April, when Miss Williams left to get married, I was offered the position permanently.'

'So you spend your days dealing with a flood of social correspondence? That must be fascinating.' The sarcasm was blatant.

There was a great deal more to it than that, but admitting that she was helping Lady Beaumont to research and write the Beaumont family history would be a dead giveaway.

Quinn slanted her a glance. 'No comment?'

'The salary's good,' she informed him tartly.

Saluting her spirit, he pursued, 'So you and Beaumont have known each other since February... Have you been engaged long?'

'You asked that before.'

'As I recall, I didn't get an answer.'

When she said nothing, he went on, 'At a guess I should say not very long at all.'

'What makes you think that?'

'You looked startled when Beaumont introduced you as his fiancée—as if you hadn't had time to get used to the idea.'

Quinn had always been a formidable opponent, she thought bitterly. He missed nothing, and his keen brain drew fast and accurate conclusions.

'In my opinion,' he went on, 'Beaumont's the conservative type, the sort to go down on one knee with a background of soft lights and sweet music and a ring ready to slip onto his chosen one's finger...'

Vexed by the open mockery, Elizabeth bit her lip.

'Yet you had no ring. Which suggested a spur-of-the-moment proposal, with the Van Hamel as a carrot. Possibly because he was unsure of you...'

The summing-up was so precise that he could almost have been there.

'Or maybe for some other reason.'

'Some other reason?'

'Either to persuade you into his bed, or to keep you there, if you were getting restive.'

If the past five years had taught Elizabeth anything, it was how to hide her feelings and exercise self-control. Slowly she began to count up to ten.

She had reached four when he invited, 'Go ahead, say it.'

'Say what?' Her voice was husky with suppressed anger.

'If you can't think of anything better, try, "How dare you?"'

'It sounds as though I'm not the only one who reads Victorian melodramas.'

He laughed as if genuinely amused. *'Touché.'* Then, like

a terrier worrying at a bone, he said, 'I gather no wedding date has yet been set?'

'No. But Richard has suggested spring.' She made her answer as offhand as possible.

'Will Lady Beaumont approve of her son's choice of future wife, do you think?' There was a bite to the question.

Elizabeth rather doubted it. Though pleasant and friendly up to a point, Lady Beaumont would almost certainly have preferred a society girl, rather than a secretary, for a daughter-in-law.

'I'm afraid I don't know,' she answered shortly. 'You'd have to ask her.'

'Suppose she *doesn't*?'

Wondering if he was trying to rattle her, Elizabeth said, 'I'd rather suppose she *does*.' Adding calmly, 'But, whether she does or not, Richard isn't a man to allow himself to be influenced.'

'So you're satisfied that he really does want to marry you?'

'He said he did.'

'And you want to marry him?'

'Of course I want to marry him.'

Quinn lifted a dark brow, and instantly she wished that rather than being so emphatic she'd simply said yes.

'Why?' he asked softly. 'Or is that a silly question?'

'You mean am I marrying him for his money?'

'Are you?'

'No.'

'Then why?'

Rattled by his persistence, she spoke the exact truth. 'I want a real home and a family.' Noting the wry twist to his lips, she added, 'Isn't that what the majority of women want?'

'So you don't love him?'

'Of course I love him.' Damn! There she was, doing it again.

'In that case I would have expected you to mention love first. The majority of women would have done.'

He was a hard man to fool.

Trying not to sound defensive, she said, 'I wouldn't have agreed to marry Richard if I didn't love him.'

Quinn laughed harshly. 'If he really loves you, the poor devil has all my sympathy.'

'I don't know what you mean,' she denied sharply.

'Oh, I think you do.'

'You're mistaken.'

He shrugged. 'I thought I detected a distinct lack of passion on your part.'

The last thing she wanted to feel was passion. Like a fire that blazed out of control, it ended up destroying everything it touched.

She fought back. 'What makes you think there's any lack of passion? In any case there's nothing *wrong* with a marriage that doesn't send both partners up in flames.'

'There's not much *right* with it.'

Stung, she cried, 'I suppose you consider you're an expert?'

'Hardly. However, if my wife—'

'But you're not married,' she burst out. Then, beset by a veritable tumult of emotion, she asked, 'Are you?'

'Yes, I'm married. What made you so sure I wasn't?'

'I-I wasn't sure… I just thought… I mean I presumed you…' The words tailed off helplessly.

He was a virile, red-blooded man and she hadn't expected him to stay celibate. Indeed she'd tortured herself with the thought of him taking a string of mistresses, and been bitterly jealous of all those unknown women. But somehow she hadn't expected him to be married.

Yet why shouldn't he be? Five years was a long time,

and he'd once said he wanted children. He might even have a family by now... The thought was like a knife twisting in her heart.

But she ought to be thankful, she told herself firmly. As far as he was concerned the past was clearly over and done with. Even if he *had* recognized her, he would no longer pose any kind of threat...

'Here we are.' Quinn's voice, holding a quiet satisfaction, broke into her thoughts.

Peering through the dense, smothering curtain of fog, Elizabeth could just make out that they were turning into Hawks Lane.

Unwilling to let Quinn know *exactly* where she lived, she had intended to get out of the car on the main road, and walk the hundred yards or so home. But now it was too late.

'What number is it?' he enquired casually.

'Fifteen,' she answered reluctantly. 'It's just past the second lamp.'

As the big car slipped down the mews like a grey ghost through the grey fog, she fumbled in her bag for her key.

When they drew up outside Cantle Cottage, she said hurriedly, 'Thank you very much for bringing me home... You needn't get out. If you drive straight on there's a turning space in about fifty yards.'

Ignoring her words, he switched off the engine and slid from behind the wheel. A moment later he was holding open her door.

In her haste to escape she stumbled and dropped the key, and heard it tinkle on the cobbles.

A hand beneath her elbow, Quinn steadied her and stooped to retrieve it.

She wondered how on earth he'd see to find it. But a moment later he was opening the door and ushering her inside.

As she switched on the wall lights and, half blocking the doorway, opened her mouth to thank him again, he calmly walked past her.

Before she knew what was happening he had closed the door against the swirling fog and was helping her off with her coat.

Having hung it in the alcove, he turned and, seeing the panic in her grey eyes, asked innocently, 'Something wrong?'

Enunciating carefully, she said, 'I'm grateful to you for bringing me home, Mr Durville, but I wasn't planing to invite you in… As I said earlier, it's been a tiring evening and I'm in need of some sleep.'

She was moving to re-open the door when his fingers closed around her wrist, his grip light but somehow relentless.

As she froze, he suggested silkily, 'Before you throw me out, I think the least you can do is offer me some coffee.'

That mocking 'before you throw me out' echoing in her ears, and knowing only too well there was no way she could make him leave until he was good and ready, she agreed stiffly, 'Very well.'

When he released her wrist, Elizabeth made herself walk in a controlled manner towards the kitchen. But somehow it still felt like a rushed escape.

Deciding instant would be quicker, she part filled the kettle and, her hands unsteady, spooned dark roast granules into a cup.

He'd always liked his coffee black and fairly strong, with just one spoonful of sugar. As soon as it was ready, she picked it up and hurried back to the living room.

The chintz curtains had been drawn across the casement windows, the standard lamp was lit, and the living-flame gas fire, which stood in the inglenook fireplace, had been turned on.

Quinn had discarded his evening jacket and loosened his bow-tie, and looked alarmingly settled and at home in shirt-sleeves, sitting on the settee in front of the leaping flames.

'Thank you.' He accepted the cup, and queried, 'Aren't you having one?'

She shook her head. 'I'm not thirsty.'

Giving her an upward glance from between thick dark lashes, he used his free hand to pat the settee beside him. 'Then come and sit by me.'

She had been intending to sit well away from him, but after a moment's hesitation, deciding it would be quicker and easier to take the line of least resistance, she obeyed, leaving as much space as possible between them.

If only he'd drink his coffee and go!

As though she'd faxed him the thought, he took a sip, and remarked, 'You must have extrasensory perception.'

When she looked at him blankly, he explained, 'You appear to know exactly how I like my coffee.'

Thrown into confusion, she lied, 'I must have been thinking of Richard. That's how he takes his... So it's just as well your tastes coincide.'

'It surprises me that a man who likes his coffee black would automatically put cream into other people's.'

Too late she recalled the creamy coffee that Richard had provided. 'He knows *I* take cream,' she said, and prayed that Quinn would let the matter drop.

Her prayer was answered.

With a slight shrug, he set his cup down on the oval coffee table, and looking around the low-ceilinged room with its white plaster walls, black beams and polished oak floorboards, commented, 'This is a real gem of a place. How long have you been living here?'

'About nine months.'

'You struck lucky. It isn't often something like this comes up for rent.'

'It isn't rented.'

'Ah!' Softly he observed, 'If one's romantically inclined, it must make an ideal love-nest.'

'If you're implying that Richard comes here—' Realising that she was playing into his hands, she broke off abruptly.

'Doesn't he?'

'Certainly not! Except to pick me up occasionally.'

Raising a dark brow, Quinn pursued, 'But he did set you up here?'

'He did no such thing!'

Quinn made no attempt to hide his scepticism. 'I wouldn't have expected anyone on a secretary's salary, even if it's an exceptionally good one, to be able to buy a place like this.'

'I didn't buy it. Emily Henderson, the writer I'd worked for for several years, asked me to take care of it...'

After living in a cramped and dingy bedsit above a seedy video shop, having the opportunity to move into Cantle Cottage had seemed like a miracle.

'She's gone to Australia for a year to stay with her son and his family,' Elizabeth added flatly, and wondered why she was taking the trouble to explain.

But she knew only too well why. It was a hangover from the past, when Quinn had so badly misjudged her. Well, the past was long gone, she reminded herself briskly, and she no longer had to justify *anything*.

Frowning, as though he could read her thoughts, he harked back, 'So where do you and Beaumont meet when you have your...shall we say...trysts? Obviously not his apartment... And I can't see the family home being at all suitable.'

Losing her temper, she snapped, 'And *I* can't see what makes *where we meet* any of your business.'

'Then you *do* sleep with him...' Though the words themselves were triumphant, there was a kind of weary accep-

tance in the low-pitched voice, rather than satisfaction.
'And he wants the Van Hamel as a carrot to keep you
where he—'

'You're quite wrong,' she broke in furiously. 'Richard
wants the Van Hamel for its own sake... And whether or
not I sleep with him is entirely my affair.'

A look that seemed to hold both anger and pain crossed
Quinn's dark face, but a split second later it was gone, and
Elizabeth knew she must have imagined it.

After a moment, his expression thoughtful, he pursued,
'Though you clearly weren't at home in the apartment, I
got the distinct impression that you were intending to stay
the night?'

'What if I was?' She tried to sound offhand.

'Yet you seemed to be unprepared, not even a sponge
bag, which leads me to believe that it hadn't been planned
in advance...

'It's my guess that he only proposed to you this evening,
perhaps on the way to the sale, and that he asked you then
to go back with him.'

Her expression telling him more clearly than words that
he was right, he smiled sardonically.

When she remained determinedly silent, he went on, 'He
was certainly *expecting* you to stay, and though he did his
best to act like a gentleman he was furious when he realized
you really were going to leave...'

Then, like a cobra striking, he asked, 'Why did you
change your mind? Was it because of me?'

'Why on earth should it be?' She made an effort to sound
dismissive.

'You tell me.'

'It was nothing to do with you,' she lied hardily.

'Then *why*?'

'I had a headache. Now, I really *would* like to go to bed,
so if you could finish your coffee...?'

Picking up his cup, he drained it, before remarking, 'My, but you seem uncommonly eager to be rid of me.'

When she made no effort to refute that statement, he turned to look at her, his green eyes gleaming. 'Bearing in mind that I still have the Van Hamel, I'm surprised you can't bring yourself to be a little more gracious.'

It was a threat, however subtly worded.

'I don't care a damn about the Van Hamel.' The retort was out before she could prevent it.

'*You* may not, but your fiancé certainly does. In fact, judging by the amount I was able to push him to tonight, I'd say he's set his heart on having it...'

Once again Quinn was one hundred per cent accurate.

'So if you don't want to see him disappointed...'

She didn't.

Possibly because of his nature and privileged upbringing, Richard wasn't a good loser. Like a spoilt child, he was unable to forget a failure. Losing the Van Hamel now would rankle, and could end up souring their whole engagement.

No matter what other precious stone he chose for her ring, Elizabeth knew quite well that, in his eyes at least, it would always be second best, and every time he looked at it he would feel angry and dissatisfied.

Gritting her teeth, she made an effort to be civil. 'I'm sorry if I've been ungracious...'

'That's better,' Quinn murmured encouragingly. 'Now perhaps you could make me some supper and another cup of coffee? Oh, and please do join me. I dislike eating alone.'

Though politely framed it was undoubtedly an order.

Knowing only too well that he was playing with her, deliberately provoking her, she felt a fierce desire to smack his mocking face and tell him to get out.

Instead, she rose to her feet without a word, and, picking up his empty cup, carried it through to the kitchen.

This time she got out the cafetière and warmed it, before taking a wholegrain loaf from the bread bin, and ham and cheese from the fridge.

She was cutting bread, when a movement in the doorway distracted her and the knife slipped and nicked her finger, making her gasp.

'Let me see.' Quinn was by her side in an instant. Lifting her hand, he examined the cut where a blob of red blood was welling.

'It's nothing,' she assured him.

All at once her stomach clenched and fire flashed through her, as he put her finger in his mouth and sucked. While he kept it there, his green eyes met and held hers, as though assessing her response.

It seemed an eternity before, head spinning, she was able to tear her gaze away.

Inspecting the now bloodless cut, he asked, 'Where do you keep your sticking-plasters?'

Trembling in every limb, and feeling as though she'd narrowly survived some disaster, she said jerkily, 'There's a first-aid box in the cupboard.'

When, with deft efficiency, he'd put a plaster on her finger and replaced the box, he remarked, 'You look shaken.' He sounded smug and self-satisfied, as if he knew perfectly well that it had nothing to do with cutting herself. 'Perhaps *I'd* better make the sandwiches?'

'No, I'm quite all right, really.' It seemed easier to be occupied.

While he leaned against one of the oak units and watched her, she finished making the sandwiches and filled the cafetière.

When it was assembled on a tray—and remembering his

'do join me' she'd added an extra plate and cup—he straightened. 'Let me carry that.'

With a sense of unreality, she followed him back to the living room.

She was about to take a seat in one of the armchairs when, having put the tray on the low table, he motioned her to sit beside him. Then, as though he owned the place, he pressed the plunger and poured coffee for them both.

Passing her a plate, he urged, 'Won't you have a sandwich?'

'Thank you.' Elizabeth took a sandwich she didn't want and toyed with it, while he began to eat with a healthy appetite.

She had presumed that, in asking for supper, he was simply demonstrating his power, but he seemed to be genuinely hungry.

Catching her look of surprise, he said, 'I missed dinner tonight.' Then he added wryly, 'You thought I was just practising being obnoxious, didn't you?'

'I didn't think you needed any practice.' The words were out before she could prevent them.

'Oh, well, I suppose I asked for that.'

To her amazement he was laughing, white, healthy teeth gleaming, deep creases appearing at each side of his chiselled mouth.

She felt her heart lurch then begin to race as she remembered the feel of that mouth touching hers...caressing her throat...finding the soft curves of her breasts...closing on a taut nipple...bringing a pleasure so exquisite it had been almost pain... Arousing a hunger that had made her shudder against him in an agony of need...

Perhaps she made some small sound, because he turned his head to look directly at her. In an instant her face flooded with scalding colour.

'Erotic thoughts?' he asked quizzically.

Knowing it was useless to deny it, she lied huskily, 'In spite of the headache I was just wishing I'd stayed with Richard.'

Hoping desperately that Quinn would believe her, she knew he *had* when his face tightened.

But why should he be angry? What she did was nothing to do with him.

Slowly, he said, 'If you can look like that when you think of him, your feelings must be a great deal more passionate than I'd imagined. I doubt if I've ever seen such naked longing on any woman's face...'

She bit her soft inner lip until she tasted blood, before saying with what equanimity she could muster, 'It's getting very late...'

Desperate for him to be gone, she jumped to her feet and, walking to the window on legs that felt like chewed string, drew back the curtain.

A grey blanket of fog pressed damply against the glass, thick and smothering, allowing no glimpse of the outside world.

As levelly as possible, she went on, 'And I'm afraid the conditions aren't improving...'

'No,' he agreed, coming to stand behind her shoulder.

Awkwardly, she went on, 'So don't you think it would make sense to—?'

'You're quite right,' he broke in smoothly. 'Rather than risk an accident, it would make more sense to stay here.'

'N-no, I didn't mean that,' she stammered. 'You can't possibly stay here. There's only one bedroom.'

'I'm quite willing to sleep on the couch.'

Panic-stricken, she cried, 'No, I don't want you to do that...'

His brows shot up. 'I see! Well, if you want me to share your bed, I'll be happy to stand in for Beaumont.'

'That wasn't what I meant!'

He sighed. 'Pity. For a moment I thought—'

'And you know quite well it wasn't.'

His grin confirming that he'd just been baiting her, he said with mock resignation, 'So the couch it is.'

With growing desperation, she clutched at straws. 'But you don't have any night things... And surely your hotel can't be too far away?'

'I *do* have some night things,' he contradicted her calmly. 'What I don't have is a hotel. You see, I hadn't planned on staying in town. My intention was to go on to Saltmarsh.'

'Saltmarsh?' The word was only a whisper.

Unbidden, her mind produced a series of vivid pictures. The town of Saltmarsh, with its narrow streets and half-timbered houses, its air of time standing still... Saltmarsh Island, some mile long by half a mile wide, connected to the mainland by a causeway which was only passable at low tide... Saltmarsh House, the beautiful old house that dominated the island...

'It's in Essex. Have you ever been there?' Quinn's glance was searching.

Her mind still full of images, she shook her head mutely.

'It was once a thriving coastal town; now it's a sleepy backwater with a population of a few thousand. My father used to live just off shore, on an island connected by a causeway.'

Used to? Henry Durville had once told her he would never willingly leave his home.

Had he become too ill to remain there? She saw Quinn's eyes narrow, and for one frightening second thought she'd asked the question aloud.

But of course she hadn't. Making an effort to pull herself together, Elizabeth went back to the real issue. 'I'm quite sure you could find a hotel. There are several not too far away.'

'I'm quite sure you're right,' he agreed easily. 'But, taking everything into consideration, I'd rather stay here.'

She found herself begging. *'No... Please...'*

'What are you so scared of? Don't you trust me not to wander in the night?'

It wasn't that. By his own admission he was married, and she was oddly convinced that he was a man who wouldn't cheat on his wife.

As she began to shake her head, he went on, 'If that's it, I promise I won't move off the couch.'

'No, it isn't.'

A gleam in his eye, he suggested, 'You're scared that with such a build-up of frustration *you'll* wander?'

'Nothing of the kind!'

'Then why are you so against me staying until morning?'

She wanted him to go *now*. *At once*. Wanted *never* to have to see him again. The thought of him being here under her roof until morning was unendurable.

Hoarsely, she said, 'Richard would be furious if he found out.'

'Then we won't tell him. Now, if you could just rustle up a spare pillow and a blanket, I'll fetch my things in.'

Shrugging into his jacket, he went out to the car, leaving the door slightly ajar.

Feeling sick and helpless, she stood rooted to the spot, watching swirls of fog drifting into the room and disappearing like wraiths in the warmer air.

A moment or two later she heard the boot lid being closed. Only then, as though some part of her mind had just kicked in, she hurried to the door and slammed it shut. If he couldn't see to drive, he could *walk* to the nearest hotel.

CHAPTER THREE

ALMOST before the thought was completed, she heard the key turn in the lock. A second later the door swung open.

Too late, she wished desperately that she'd reacted quicker and either pushed home the bolt or set the safety chain.

Closing the door carefully behind him, Quinn put the small grip he was carrying down beside the settee, and shook his head reprovingly. 'That wasn't very kind. It's just as well I had the key in my pocket.'

'Was that chance or foresight?' she asked bitterly.

'I try not to leave too much to chance...'

So the first time he'd opened the door he'd kept her key. She'd had so much on her mind she hadn't given a thought to what might have happened to it.

'Which is just as well. It's as thick as soup out there. Even trying to walk to the nearest hotel would have been no picnic.'

Deliberately, he stepped towards her. 'Don't you think you owe me an apology?'

'No, I don't,' she retorted with a boldness she was far from feeling. Then, standing her ground with an effort, she added, 'I didn't invite you in in the first place, and I want you to go.'

'I'm afraid it's what *I* want that counts.' Though he spoke quietly, there was little doubt that beneath his air of calm he was furiously angry.

He took another step, and all at once he was much too near. She saw, as though magnified by some glass in her mind, that his dark hair was dewed with tiny droplets, his

41

lashes were long and curly, and his green eyes had flecks of gold in their depths. At the corner of his mouth a muscle twitched spasmodically.

As she stood staring into that tough, dynamic face, he took her head between his hands.

She froze. Afraid he was going to kiss her. *Wanting* him to kiss her.

Even after all this time, and remembering how he'd cruelly shattered her life, part of her still hungered for him with a deep, primitive desire that frightened her half to death.

One hand dropping to cradle the warmth of her nape, the fingers of the other following the curve of her cheek and tracing the neat contours of her ear, he leaned closer.

Her lips parted and, drowning in a wave of emotion, she waited.

But instead of kissing her he tugged at first one earlobe, then the other.

She saw him slip something into his pocket but, dazed and disorientated, it was a second or two before she realized he had deftly removed her earrings.

'What are you...?' The slurred words were lost and every thought went out of her head as he nuzzled her ear, exploring the neat whorls with the tip of his tongue, making her shudder.

Firm and sensual, his lips travelled along the line of her jaw to find and linger at the warm hollow at the base of her other ear. While she stood spellbound, his teeth nipped playfully at the lobe, before that marauding mouth began to move towards hers.

At last. She closed her eyes.

His lips reached the corner of her mouth and lingered there tantalizingly. She was waiting in an agony of suspense, when suddenly he lifted his head and moved away, leaving her bereft.

Her eyes flew open.

He was watching her with a taunting little smile. 'In view of what I said earlier about not moving off the couch, it might be better to call a halt before things get too heated.'

'Why did you do that?' she asked jerkily.

'Don't you know?'

'Because you were angry?'

He raised a dark brow. 'You think it was meant to be a punishment?'

'Wasn't it?'

'Suppose we call it an experiment.'

'An experiment?'

'I wanted to find out just how much you *do* care about Beaumont...'

Watching her bite her lip, he added softly, 'And I'd say not a great deal.'

'How did you reach that conclusion?'

Quinn smiled. 'If you can stop thinking about him and react to me in that way...'

'It hasn't occurred to you that I might have reacted as I did because I *was* thinking about him?'

She had the satisfaction of seeing that mocking smile vanish and his mouth tighten.

'In any case I don't see that what I feel about Richard is any concern of yours.

Discarding his jacket once more, he said, 'Well, if I'm giving up the Van Hamel, I have a kind of vested interest.'

All her earlier doubts surfaced in a rush.

Without pausing to think, she asked, 'Are you really prepared to let Richard have the diamond? Or is this some kind of game?'

'I'm quite prepared to let him have it,' Quinn said evenly.

'Why, when you went to so much trouble to outbid him? It makes no sense.'

'The diamond doesn't matter. It was just the means to an end.'

Determined to have some answers, she persisted, 'Then what *does* matter? Why are you here? What's the point of all this?'

'Haven't you guessed, Jo?'

For a second or two shock made her head spin, there was a roaring in her ears, and faintness threatened to overwhelm her.

Watching her lose every last trace of colour, Quinn said abruptly, 'You'd better sit down.'

He steered her to the nearest chair and, pushing her into it, sat down opposite, so he could see her face. 'Do you really believe I wouldn't remember you?'

No, perhaps she had never really *believed* it. But, reassured to some extent by Quinn's apparent lack of recognition, she had clung to a forlorn hope, played out the charade he had instigated, because she had been frightened to face the reality.

Somehow she found her voice, and answered obliquely, 'It all happened a long time ago, and we were only together a very short time.'

'But *you* remembered *me*.'

She'd tried hard to forget him, but she knew now she would never succeed. While ever she lived, he would be part of her very being.

Her eyes were drawn to his face and held there as though mesmerized. In looks alone, the years hadn't altered him. The only difference was an air of added maturity, lines of control and self-discipline around his mouth, that made him even more fascinating and formidable.

If Quinn had been inordinately attractive then, now he was even more so. He would still be good-looking and charismatic at eighty.

'See any difference?' he enquired mockingly.

She shook her head. 'You haven't altered at all. I've altered a great deal.'

'Including your name.' Then he said slowly, 'You used to be as pretty as a picture. Now you have a kind of poignant beauty... But I never doubted you were the same woman.'

'If you recognized me straight away, why didn't you say something?'

'I was curious as to how things were. It was quite obvious you hadn't told Beaumont about me.'

'There was no reason to tell him,' she said, and was aware that she sounded defensive.

'I would have thought there was one very good reason.'

She half shook her head. 'In the circumstances I decided the past was better left behind.'

That was only part of the truth. She had shied away from talking about Quinn. It was like tearing open old, but still unhealed, wounds.

'Even though you'd agreed to marry him?'

'You were right in presuming we hadn't been engaged long. Richard only proposed to me on the way to Belham House. I'd had no time to think things through or decide how much to tell him.'

His green eyes thoughtful, Quinn pursued, 'But when I appeared on the scene and Beaumont began to introduce us, why didn't you admit then that we knew each other?'

Elizabeth looked down at her hands clenched in her lap. 'You treated me like a stranger and I hoped...I hoped I wouldn't need to...'

'Considering our relationship, quite a deception to embark on.'

Helplessly, she tried to explain. 'I was already committed. Until a few minutes before, I hadn't had the faintest idea that you and he had ever met'

'But you knew I was in the saleroom?'

'Yes... Though when Richard wanted to know who was bidding against him I pretended I couldn't see. Then your name was mentioned...

'There was obviously no love lost between you, and in view of what had happened over the diamond, when he asked if I knew you, I panicked and said no.'

'I see,' Quinn said. Then, his voice sharp, he asked, 'Has he always known you as Elizabeth Cavendish?'

'Yes.'

'Why *Cavendish*?'

She lifted her head. 'It was the name of a schoolfriend.'

'When did you change it?'

'When your detective caught up with me.'

'You sound bitter.'

'I have every right to be bitter.'

'That's a matter of opinion. Why did you run out on me, Jo?'

'Don't call me Jo.' It brought the past much too close.

'Tell me why?' he persisted.

'I told you in my note.'

'Tell me again.'

'Because I realized I'd made a terrible mistake.'

'There had to be more to it than that,' he said flatly. 'But instead of waiting to talk to me you ran like a frightened rabbit the minute my back was turned...'

Grimly, he asked, 'Did you really think I'd let you go so easily?'

'Why not? You had achieved what you'd set out to do.'

His eyes narrowed. 'Oh? And what exactly was that?'

Cursing her unruly tongue, she lifted her chin and said, 'I realized, rather belatedly, that you'd only married me to save your father from my clutches.'

'One rich man in exchange for another?' Softly, he probed, 'Now what, or *who*, put that idea into your head?'

Unable to tell him the truth, she used attack as the best means of defence. 'Do you deny it?'

'Is there any point in denying it?'

Then, like a whiplash, he said, 'Tell me, Jo, do you deny angling for a wealthy husband?'

'Is there any point in denying it?' she retorted.

He smiled bleakly. 'So why didn't you stay with me? Why ask for the marriage to be annulled without even sampling the good life?'

Wanting to hurt him as much as he'd hurt her, she said, 'I decided that staying with you was too high a price to pay.'

'Don't you mean you got scared? When, somehow, you discovered I knew all about your little games, you were afraid to stay.'

'If by "little games" you mean I'd have designs on Henry, it wasn't true. You were mistaken.'

'I don't think so. Though you had a look of radiant innocence, you'd battened on to my father like a leech, and if I hadn't taken a hand you'd have sucked him dry.'

Elizabeth shuddered.

'Perhaps you imagined that, living in the States, I was too distant to either know or care what was going on? But for Piery's sake, as well as my father's, I felt the need to do something.'

'But if that's what you thought, why didn't you simply warn me off?' *That she might have coped with.* 'Why go to all the trouble of marrying me?' *That was the unbearable part.*

His eyes cold and cruel, he said, 'I couldn't be sure you'd go. My father was in love with you, so you had a powerful hold. Marrying you, even if we didn't stay together, seemed to offer a permanent solution.'

'You keep saying Henry was in love with me, but it wasn't that kind of relationship at all. *Truly* it wasn't...'

Oh, what was the use? Quinn thought she was a gold-digger and she'd never convince him otherwise.

As though to prove the point, he said, 'Tell me, when you decided to leave me, why didn't you try to negotiate some kind of financial settlement?'

'I didn't want your money. All I wanted was my freedom.'

'Then why didn't you wait to see me and ask me for it?'

'Because I didn't *want* to see you...'

Knowing just *why* he'd married her, and bitterly ashamed of what a *naïve* fool she'd been, she hadn't been able to bear the thought of facing him.

'I hoped I'd never have to set eyes on you again.'

'Whereas, for all these years, I've been hoping quite the opposite.'

'But why? I don't understand *why*.'

'Perhaps because nothing was settled between us, and I don't like leaving unfinished business.'

His voice harsh, he demanded, 'Did you imagine changing your name would make any difference? I would have found you no mater how long it took.'

'You don't mean you've had detectives looking all this time—' she smiled tauntingly '—then we meet up quite by chance?'

'Not *quite* by chance,' he said silkily.

As his meaning sank in, her eyes widened. 'You *knew* I'd be at the sale?'

'I *hoped* you'd be there. I'd seen a list of the "Specially Invited" and Beaumont's name was on it.'

'But how did you...?'

Quinn smiled a shade wryly. 'This is where chance *does* come in. Piery spotted you...'

Piery, Quinn's young half-brother, whom she had always thought of as her friend...

'He paid a brief visit to one of Lady Beaumont's big

charity functions, and he happened to catch sight of you with Beaumont...

'At least he *thought* it was you, but wasn't sure. Luckily, that night there was a photograph of the pair of you in one of the society columns. He tore it out and sent it to me. That's why I dropped everything and came over for the sale.'

Despite the warmth of the fire, she shivered. 'What if I hadn't been there?'

Quinn's shoulders lifted in a slight shrug. 'I would have had to make other plans. Once I knew I could find you through Beaumont it ceased to be a major problem.

'Though I must admit I was pleased when I caught sight of you sitting with him. It made things so much simpler. All I needed to do was wait and see what he was bidding for...'

'And make sure you outbid him,' he said resentfully.

'Exactly. I wanted some kind of bait. Something that would give me an opening.'

'I see what you meant when you said the diamond was just the means to an end.'

He smiled. 'In the event, things worked out even better than I'd dared hope. If you had told Beaumont the truth, or admitted to knowing me, he would no doubt have been a great deal more cautious.'

Now it was too late she wished fervently that she *had* brought things into the open. If she'd acted differently, she wouldn't be in the nerve-racking position of having Quinn here, an unwanted and dangerous guest in her own home...

Breaking into her thoughts, the grandmother clock to the left of the fireplace chimed twelve-thirty.

Getting to his feet, he stretched, supple as any cat, and reached to turn off the lights, leaving only the standard lamp and the glow from the leaping flames.

'It's been a long day so, now I've answered your questions, if you want to—'

'But you haven't,' she broke in wildly. 'You still haven't told me *why* you went to all this trouble. What do you mean by *unfinished business*...'

He turned his head to look at her. His face was partly shadowed, but little flames danced in his eyes. Softly, he said, 'My dear Jo, surely you know?'

'I wish you wouldn't call me that,' she muttered. 'And no, I don't know.'

He sighed theatrically. 'You never used to be obtuse. As I recall, you were quick and intelligent and more often than not on my wavelength...'

'Then I'm not any longer. I just don't see what you hope to gain... Why you're here...' She made a helpless gesture with her hands. 'You're married, I'm soon going to be, and—'

'And your fiancé won't like the idea of me spending the night with you?'

Ignoring the provocative phrasing, she said curtly, 'I've already told you he won't. Will your wife?'

Sitting down again, he smiled tauntingly. 'She doesn't seem to.'

It took a moment or two for the implication to sink in. Her throat feeling as though a silken noose had tightened round it, Elizabeth whispered hoarsely, 'You don't...' Swallowing hard, she tried again. 'You don't mean that I'm...?'

'Still my wife? That's exactly what I mean.'

'No, I *can't* be,' she cried desperately. 'The marriage was going to be annulled.'

'That was your idea. You didn't wait to see if I was in agreement.'

'But when I swore I had no intention of living with you

the family lawyers drew up the necessary papers and I signed them.'

'Well, *I* didn't.'

'Why?' It wasn't as if he'd ever loved her. 'Your lawyers agreed it was the best thing to do.'

'*I* didn't happen to think so.' Frowning, he went on, 'Though when time passed and I couldn't trace you one of the things I was afraid of was that you might presume it *had* been annulled and marry again.'

A note of satisfaction in his voice, he added, 'It appears I found you in the nick of time. Bigamy is a serious offence.'

'But ours wasn't a proper marriage...'

'You mean it hasn't been consummated?'

Colour creeping into her face, she lifted her chin defiantly. 'It hadn't.'

'No,' he agreed pleasantly. 'Though I'm afraid, as things stand, that fact doesn't make us legally any less married.'

As though somehow, miraculously, it would wipe out the past and put everything right, she protested, 'But I've promised to marry Richard.'

'Somewhat prematurely, as it turns out.'

Still unwilling to believe it, she cried, 'You didn't say anything when he was talking about an engagement ring.'

His smile sardonic, Quinn asked, 'Would you have preferred me to tell him that he was wasting his time because you were still my wife?'

She winced.

'I thought not.' Then he said briskly, 'However, as you mentioned a spring wedding, he'll have to know soon.'

Putting a distracted hand to her head, she whispered, 'How am I ever going to tell him?'

'Is he aware you've been married?'

'No.' She barely breathed the word.

'Then however you tell him it's bound to come as something of a shock.'

Quinn sounded callous, uncaring, but a moment later that was proved false when he remarked, 'I feel sorry for the poor devil.'

'Oh, *why* didn't you get an annulment?' Elizabeth was suddenly close to tears. 'It would have been all over and done with. Now it's going to hurt Richard, and disrupt all our lives.'

'So you still want an annulment?'

'Of course I do.'

'And if *I* don't?'

Her blood ran cold. 'But you *must* do. While you're tied to a woman you haven't seen for over five years, *you're* not free to marry again.'

'What makes you think I want to?'

'You once said you'd like a family… Surely that means marrying again?'

'Suppose, having made one lot of marriage vows, I regard them as sacred?'

'Don't try to tell me you meant any of those vows,' Elizabeth cried passionately. 'The whole thing was—' She broke off and bit her lip.

After a moment she drew a deep, steadying breath and went on with icy determination, 'If you don't agree to an annulment, then *I'll* take whatever steps are necessary to end the marriage.'

'Really?' he laughed, teeth gleaming in the firelight. 'That sounds rather like a mouse threatening to bite a cat.'

'But I won't be on my own.' She made no effort to hide the triumph. 'Richard will be with me all the way.'

At the mention of Richard, she saw Quinn's face darken with a look of jealous fury.

No, she must have misread it. He couldn't be *jealous*. To be jealous he would need to feel something positive for her, and there was little doubt that he felt nothing but cold resentment. Still, he could be, and undoubtedly was, possessive.

Proving she was right, he said brusquely, 'As you remarked earlier there's no love lost between myself and Beaumont, so do you seriously think I'll let him have what's mine?'

'I'm *not* yours,' she denied sharply. 'In any event I don't see how you can stop him. If you try to put up any opposition, Richard had more than enough wealth and power to fight you.'

'Yes, I must congratulate you on managing to hook another rich man...'

Elizabeth flinched as though he'd slapped her.

Smiling mirthlessly, Quinn went on, 'But when you've told him the truth, will he be willing to *use* all that wealth and power? Will he still *want* to go ahead with the wedding when he knows just whose wife you are?'

Richard had said he loved her, but would he still want to marry her when he knew how she had lied and deceived him? When he knew she was Quinn Durville's wife?

But she *wasn't* Quinn's wife, she reminded herself urgently. A ten-minute ceremony and a marriage certificate didn't make her a wife, any more than five years spent apart made a happy marriage.

'I'm sure he will.' She spoke over-emphatically in an attempt to hide any doubts.

'You seem very certain.'

'I am certain.'

'What if he *did* change his mind?' Quinn pressed.

'I'd still want to be free as soon as possible.'

'Very well.' His voice was matter-of-fact, his face devoid of emotion. 'We'll talk about it in the morning.'

Knowing Quinn wasn't a man to throw in the towel, she felt a sudden unease, his apparent capitulation worrying her almost more than continued opposition would have done. But she mustn't let him see it.

Getting to her feet, she muttered, 'I'll fetch some bed-clothes.'

When she returned with a couple of pillows and a small pile of blankets, she found he had removed his tie and was just finishing unbuttoning his evening shirt. As she crossed the room, he pulled it free from the waistband of his trousers, and tossed it over a chair.

His broad chest and shoulders were smoothly muscled, and in the firelight his clear olive skin gleamed like oiled silk. A scattering of crisp, dark body hair vee'd down to a trim waist and lean hips.

Her mouth went dry.

She dropped the bedclothes on to the settee and turned to escape, only to find that, either by accident or design, he was blocking her way.

Looking anywhere but at him, she managed, 'There are plenty of towels in the bathroom cupboard. If you want anything else let me know.'

'To save me wandering into your room by mistake, I'd better check where the bathroom is.'

Steadfastly ignoring the first half of the sentence, she told him, 'It's the door facing you at the end of the landing. You can use it first.'

Without moving, he said lazily, 'Then I'll say good-night.'

'Goodnight.'

She made to brush past him, and gasped as his fingers closed lightly around her arm. 'You said if I wanted any-thing else...'

He smiled into her wide, scared eyes, and traced her mouth with his free hand, gently parting her lips to rub the pad of his thumb over her pearly teeth. 'Do you have a spare toothbrush? I seem to have mislaid mine.'

'There's one in the bathroom cabinet.' Tearing herself free, she fled.

'Sleep well.' His mocking injunction followed her up the stairs.

Damn him! Elizabeth thought furiously, as she hurried into her room and closed the door. He'd done that deliberately to rout and unsettle her.

During the past couple of years she'd almost managed to convince herself that the chemistry between them couldn't have been nearly as powerful as she'd imagined; that if they ever met again it would be gone and she would be free.

But, shaken to the soul, she was forced to admit that she'd been abysmally wrong; it was still there, drawing her as strongly as ever. And, despite her attempts to pretend otherwise, he almost certainly knew it. That was the real danger...

Her mind a mass of seething emotions, she had just started to undress when she heard the stair treads creak beneath Quinn's weight, and his light footsteps on the oak-floored landing.

She waited, her heart in her mouth. After a second or two she heard the bathroom door open and close, then, faintly, the sound of running water as the shower was turned on.

Breathing a sigh of relief, she finished undressing, pulled on her nightie and, sitting at her dressing-table, began to take the pins from her hair.

In the mirror her oval face appeared pale and pinched, and her eyes, a clear dark grey with no hint of blue, held a look of trepidation, as if seeing Quinn again had killed all her hard-won confidence.

Five years ago, ensnared by a sexuality of such dark power that she had been unable to free herself, she had

thought that loving him, wanting him, was the most wonderful thing that had ever happened to her.

Instead, it had almost destroyed her.

Could still destroy her...

As she shied away from the thought, she heard him leave
the bathroom. A few seconds later she froze as, instead of
going on to the stairs, his footsteps stopped outside her
door.

All the internal doors had old-fashioned wooden latches
and boasted neither locks nor bolts. Suppose he just walked
in?

She was holding her breath when his knuckles rapped
gently against the wood.

'What do you want?' Even to her own ears her voice
sounded thin and scared.

'Just letting you know the bathroom's free.'

Elizabeth felt sure she heard him laugh softly as he carried on down the stairs.

When she'd pulled herself together enough to venture
out, everything was quiet and the living room was in darkness.

Somewhat reassured, she washed her face and hands and
cleaned her teeth before going to bed.

Her bedroom curtains hadn't been drawn across, and
Elizabeth opened reluctant eyes to a grey morning that still
held lingering traces of fog.

As, dazed and anxious, she wondered what had jolted
her from sleep, the memory of the previous night suddenly
flooded back, explaining the feeling of apprehension that
lay like a weight on her mind.

But before she could get her thoughts into any kind of
order there was a tap at the door. She jerked upright just
as it opened to admit Quinn carrying a tray of tea and toast.

He was wearing well-cut casual trousers and an olive-green sweater. Freshly showered and shaved, his dark hair parted on the left and brushed back, his eyes clear and sparkling with health, he looked breathtakingly handsome and virile.

'Good morning.' His greeting sounded easy, almost friendly.

Her mouth compressed, she said, 'I'd rather you didn't just walk in like that.'

'I did knock,' he pointed out. 'Twice. And as we're married it's quite decent.'

When she refused to rise to the bait, he queried, 'I hope you slept well?'

This time she did rise, answering decidedly and quite untruthfully, 'Very well.'

With so much on her mind she had been unable to settle, and, thoughts going round and round like an unstoppable carousel, she had tossed and turned restlessly until the early hours of the morning.

Only when a grey dawn was filtering in, and she could hear the faint sounds of London stirring into life, had she slept.

Stooping, he settled the tray across her knees.

'Thank you.' Her voice was cool and dismissive, and her glance at the door said clearly, *I'd like you to go now*.

Choosing to ignore her tacit request, he sat down on the edge of the bed and reached to pour the tea.

For the first time she noticed the tray was set for two. Hurriedly, she said, 'I'd prefer you to take it back and I'll come downstairs.'

Putting his own cup on the bedside table, he raised a quizzical brow. 'I presume that's because I'm planning to join you?'

'I'd rather you didn't.'

He studied the tumble of dark silky hair, the demure nightdress. 'There's no need to worry; after all, I'm fully dressed, and you look positively Victorian.'

When she said nothing, he asked ironically, 'Don't you and Beaumont ever have breakfast in bed?'

'I don't eat in bed as a rule,' she informed him coldly.

'Then make this an exception.' He reached for the toast rack.

She watched his long, lean hands as he began to butter the crisp, golden toast, and remembered them touching her, caressing her, moving over her body with sensuous appreciation, bringing a singing delight wherever they touched.

'Marmalade or honey?'

His query made her jump. She took a deep, gasping breath, like a swimmer who'd been under water too long. 'I don't want any toast.'

Carefully, he said, 'If you're still set on ending our marriage, we need to talk, and over breakfast is as good a time as any.'

His light tone failing to disguise his air of purpose, he added, 'As I've mentioned before, I don't like eating alone... So may I suggest you decide between marmalade and honey, and start drinking your tea before it gets cold?'

It seemed that in this, as in most things, he intended to have his way.

'Marmalade,' she said, and picked up her cup. The sooner they had talked, the sooner he would leave.

As though she'd spoken the thought aloud, he remarked, 'I don't want to be too late getting away. I'm going to Saltmarsh. You remember Saltmarsh?'

'Yes,' she admitted in a stifled voice.

'You didn't seem to last night.'

He appeared to be waiting for a response of some kind, and as though the words were dragged out of her she found herself saying, 'I've never been back there.'

'Not even when my father was desperately ill and asking to see you.'

'I—I didn't know...'

'It seems he moved heaven and earth to try to find you.'

'Is he...?'

'He died six months ago.'

Elizabeth swallowed hard. 'I'm sorry.' Then, lifting her chin, she added, 'Whether you believe it or not, I was genuinely fond of him.'

That was less than the truth. In the comparatively short time she had been Henry Durville's secretary he had become like a father to her.

'The regard appears to have been mutual,' Quinn observed wryly. 'He left you half his estate.... His solicitors have been trying to trace you.'

CHAPTER FOUR

ELIZABETH'S jaw dropped. *'What?'*

'He left you half his estate,' Quinn repeated flatly.

'Are you *sure*?' She felt stunned.

'Quite sure. Surprisingly, as we hadn't been on speaking terms since you ran away, he made me his executor...

'Apart from Saltmarsh House and some family jewellery, which was willed to me, and a substantial legacy for his housekeeper, everything was split between you and Piery.'

'Oh, no,' she whispered. If she'd ever treasured any faint hope of convincing Quinn he'd been wrong about her, it had just died.

Lifting a face that looked ashen, she insisted, 'I don't want his money. I never did want it. You can have it back. He should have left it to you in the first place.'

Quinn shook his head. 'Even if we hadn't fallen out he knew perfectly well that I had no need of it.'

'Then Piery must have it.'

'Piery has quite enough.' Seeing she was about to protest, Quinn went on, 'If it puts your mind at rest, *I* made sure Piery was financially secure when Henry turned him out.'

Startled, she asked, 'Why on earth did Henry turn *Piery* out? What had *he* done?'

'During the bust-up, he actually used the phrase "There's no fool like an old fool" in front of Henry.'

'You don't mean Piery thought...?'

'That Henry was besotted? What else was he to think?'

Oh, dear God, Elizabeth thought despairingly, it was worse than she'd ever imagined. Wringing her hands, she burst out, 'Well, I don't care who the money goes to, but *I* won't take it.'

A cynical twist to his lips, Quinn said, 'You may change your mind if Beaumont changes his.'

'If I don't marry Richard I'm quite capable of supporting myself.'

'I don't doubt it. But Henry left you that money. He *wanted* you to have it.'

'No, I can't take it.'

'Then you'll have to contact his solicitors and tell them how to dispose of it. In the meantime,' he added carefully, 'there's one item of jewellery that I hope you'll be prepared to accept.'

Seeing she was about to refuse, he continued, 'When Henry was on his deathbed—'

'You were there?'

'They sent for both Piery and myself. Though the family had been split for so long it seemed he wanted to make it up before he died.

'Unfortunately, by the time we got there, a further stroke, in a series of strokes, meant he was unable to speak or write intelligibly. But he made me understand that he wanted *you* to have this particular brooch. So if you *did* think anything of him...' Quinn left the sentence unfinished.

'Who did it belong to?'

'When I did a spot of delving I found it had been in the family since the early sixteen hundreds. I presume that, as you were helping my father write the family history, you know that the Durvilles first made their fortune as shipbuilders and shipowners before becoming merchant bankers?'

'Yes.'

Watching her face like a hawk, he continued, 'Well, it seems the brooch belonged to the wife of Christopher

Durville, who helped to build, and actually sailed with, the *Mayflower*.'

'Oh, but I couldn't take anything as—'

'Before you start to argue, may I point out that it's probably *because* of its historical connections that he wanted you to have it? And there are no other close female relatives who might conceivably want it.

'As you probably know, Henry had only the one brother, my mother has been dead for well over twenty years, and Piery's mother ran away with another man.'

With a bleak smile, he added, 'For one reason or another we seem unable to keep our women in this family.'

Wincing at his bitterness, she said, 'Though I'm not really a relative, if Henry wanted to give me the brooch, I'll be pleased to have it.'

A look that she was unable to decipher crossed Quinn's dark face. 'Then as soon as you're ready we'll go.'

Startled, she asked, 'Go? Go where?'

'Saltmarsh.'

'No, I can't go with you.'

She couldn't bring herself to return to the place where once, before the bottom had dropped out of her world, she'd been so very happy.

'Apart from picking up the brooch, there are some other things I'd like you to look through.'

'I don't really—'

'All of them belong to you.'

As she began to shake her head, he said, 'Because everything happened so quickly, you left quite a few personal possessions at the house.'

In a stifled voice, she said, 'Perhaps you could let me have the brooch. There's nothing else I want.'

'Nothing?'

'Nothing at all.'

His face hardened. 'Are you sure about that? I can give you—'

Feeling unbearably pressured, she cried a shade wildly, 'I've told you, I don't want anything else from you.'

'Not even that freedom you were on about?'

She caught her breath. 'Do you mean you'll be willing to have the marriage annulled?'

He glanced at her from beneath long, dark lashes. 'I might be. On one condition.'

'What condition?'

'That you come down to Saltmarsh with me.'

Why was he so determined to have her go with him to Saltmarsh? Elizabeth wondered with a shiver. What could he hope to gain? Maybe nothing. Perhaps it was simply to feed his ego, to prove his power over her?

Well, whatever his reasons, she wouldn't go, wouldn't allow him to blackmail her like this. She would call his bluff and tell him to do his worst.

But if he *wasn't* bluffing, though he couldn't *prevent* her getting an annulment, he could no doubt make things lengthy and difficult...

Watching the conflicting emotions chase across her face, Quinn said levelly, 'The choice is yours.'

Unable to make it, Elizabeth found herself playing for time. 'Who lives there now?'

'Only the housekeeper. After my father died I let the rest of the staff go.' Casually, Quinn went on, 'Before I return home I'm hoping to get the place cleared of all personal stuff.'

With a sudden feeling of dismay, she asked sharply, 'Surely you don't mean you're thinking of putting it up for sale?'

'Why not? Other than the housekeeper, who's been at Saltmarsh House for the past thirty years, no one seems interested in living there. And thanks to the legacy my father left her Mrs Wickstead will soon be able to retire comfortably.

'When Piery got married—'

'Piery got married?'

'Three months ago, to Gemma Buchan, the youngest daughter of Lord Buchan.'

So that explained why Piery had been at the charity do, Elizabeth thought irrelevantly; Lady Beaumont and Lady Buchan were old friends.

'As I was saying,' Quinn went on, 'when Piery got married I offered to give him Saltmarsh House. But he has to be in town most days, and he didn't think commuting was practicable. I can't say I blame him. However, it does mean that the house is standing virtually empty.'

'But why sell it? You can't need the money.'

'What's the point of keeping it?'

'Henry would never have parted with it. He loved the old place...'

Then, with a kind of desperation, she said, 'Doesn't the fact that it's been in the Durville family for generations mean anything to you? I know you've chosen to live in the States for most of your life, but surely you—'

'Do you know *why* I chose to live in the States?' Quinn broke in curtly.

She shook her head.

'Then perhaps it's time I told you about my childhood. When my mother and father met, she was eighteen and he was thirty-three. To all intents and purposes he was a confirmed bachelor, but a few weeks later they were married.

'She died when I was just four and a half, leaving my father and me alone. The following autumn he met and fell deeply in love with a dark-haired slip of a girl called Beth. She refused to marry him, but she agreed to come and live with us. She was beautiful and kind and I worshipped her.

I felt sure she loved me, and I was just starting to feel secure again when one day she kissed me goodbye and left.

'The following year, and probably out of loneliness, my father married a redhead named Helen. But this time things were very different. I disliked my new stepmother, and she disliked me.

'I can't say I blame her; I was an awkward, surly child, and jealous as hell…'

Why had Quinn elected to tell her all that, Elizabeth wondered helplessly, when it was no longer any concern of hers…?

But he was going on. 'When Piery was born, things went from bad to worse. He seemed to get all the attention, and, feeling even more unloved and unwanted, I became almost impossible to live with.

'One day, when I'd been particularly difficult, Helen told my father that she couldn't stand it any longer. Either I went or she did.'

Quinn, who had been speaking quite dispassionately, smiled bleakly at Elizabeth's appalled expression.

'Oh, yes, I was young and foolish enough to hope he might want to keep me. It wasn't until I got a lot older that I realized what an impossible situation he'd been faced with.

'In the event he decided that, young as I was, the only thing he could do was pack me off to a boarding-school. But then my uncle William, who had joined the Boston branch of the family and married an American, offered to take me for a while. My father gave me the choice, and I chose to go to Boston.

'It was a happy choice. My aunt and uncle, who hadn't been able to have a family of their own, gave me the kind of love and care every child needs, and became in effect my parents.

'When Helen left Piery and my father for another man,

they asked me if I wanted to go home. I said no. As far as I was concerned, Boston *was* my home. I didn't come back to England, not even for a visit, until I was grown up.'

His voice holding a hint of challenge, he asked, 'Now do you still expect me to care about the house?'

'I can quite understand how you might still be angry and embittered,' Elizabeth said carefully.

'Ah, but I'm not. And don't go thinking I hated either Piery or my father…'

A sudden bleakness assailed her. No, recalling what he'd done to help and protect them, she would never have thought that.

'Though after all those years we were virtual strangers and we all had hang-ups—I felt resentful, my father felt guilty, and Piery was jealous in his turn—we soon got on very well.

'By the time you came on the scene, though we didn't meet often, we were as close as any normal family.'

And unwittingly she had wrecked that closeness.

A razor-sharp edge to his tone, Quinn added, 'Though perhaps that's hardly the right word to use in connection with our family. It isn't *normal* for a father and son to fall in love with the same woman.'

'And it isn't true!'

'You can't deny that my father was in love with you… And even I, who in the circumstances ought to have had a great deal more sense, ended up totally bewitched.'

But that was a complete misinterpretation. Henry had been *fond* of her, which wasn't the same as being in love; and Quinn, despite what he'd just said, had never cared twopence for her.

'It isn't true,' she repeated.

'Isn't it?'

Elizabeth felt hopeless and defeated. What was the point of arguing? It was just a waste of breath. Wearily, she said,

'Anyway, it's all over and done with. Henry's gone, and our marriage will soon be annulled.'

His smile enigmatic, he reminded her, 'That depends on whether or not you come to Saltmarsh with me.'

Every atom of her being rebelled at the thought. How could she *bear* to go back and stir up all the painful memories that lay in wait there? Especially with Quinn watching her, aware of everything she was thinking and feeling.

But for Richard's sake, as well as her own, she wanted everything to be smooth and straightforward. It was even conceivable that if things moved quickly enough she would be free in time to plan a spring wedding.

Supposing Richard was still willing to marry her when he knew the truth.

Though whether he was or not, Elizabeth thought decidedly, she wanted this mockery of a marriage to be over and done with. Wanted Quinn out of her life as soon as possible.

If, to achieve that, she had to give in to his demands and go with him, then she would do it. They would only be there a short while, and Mrs Wickstead, a comfortable, homely woman, was still living in the house, so they wouldn't be alone...

Taking a deep breath, she agreed, 'Very well, I'll come,' and watched for any overt sign of triumph.

But, his face impassive, he said, 'As you may recall, it has to be low tide to get across the causeway, so to be on the safe side we'd better not lose any time.'

Carefully, she suggested, 'Then if you wouldn't mind waiting downstairs I'll be as quick as I can.'

Smiling wryly at her studious politeness, he picked up the tray, and a moment later the latch clicked behind him.

Hurrying to the bathroom, Elizabeth cleaned her teeth and showered. When she returned to the bedroom she found the pillows and neatly folded blankets Quinn had used the previous night piled at the foot of her bed.

As quickly as possible, she coiled up her hair and dressed to make a statement, all the while striving to persuade herself that she was doing the right thing. But, some sixth sense warning of danger, she was unable to dispel an inner conviction that she was acting like a fool.

When she made her way downstairs, Quinn was nowhere to be seen. Opening the door, she found that he was waiting by the car. Wearing an olive-green jacket over his sweater, his dark hair curling a little in the damp, misty air, he looked much younger than his thirty-two years, and disturbingly attractive.

Feeling her heart rate quicken, she made an effort to pull herself together while his gaze travelled over her, taking in her businesslike grey suit and silk blouse, her smart leather court shoes and shoulder-bag, her neat chignon.

A glint in his eye, he commented, 'I can see you're all dressed for a casual day at the coast.'

Ignoring the sarcasm, she asked levelly, 'Do you still have my key?' and breathed a sigh of relief when he handed it over like a lamb.

He would no doubt bring her home, and this time she would take care, not only to keep him on the doorstep, but to retain possession of the key.

Dropping it into her bag, she closed the door behind her, and let him help her into the front passenger seat of the Mercedes.

Only as they were drawing away did she realize that she'd forgotten to replace her watch. Oh, well, it was too late to go back now.

Traffic seemed especially heavy, and it took them longer to get clear of London than might have been anticipated. But, in spite of his earlier stated wish not to lose any time, once they were under way Quinn showed no sign of impatience.

His well-shaped hands easy on the wheel, he drove in silence as they headed north-east through an unremarkable countryside of low plateaus with rugged edges.

Uncomfortably aware of him, of that muscular thigh so close to hers, she stared fixedly out of the window.

'Fascinating scenery,' Quinn remarked sardonically.

She lifted her softly rounded chin. 'I like Essex.'

'Did you like living on Saltmarsh island with a boy of eighteen and an elderly man in a wheelchair?'

Gritting her teeth, she refused to answer.

Quinn gave her a sidelong glance and changed tack. 'As you were helping Henry dig out the family history I suppose you know a fair bit about the island?'

She strove to speak evenly. 'I know that over the centuries, though there's no record of more than the one dwelling on it, the seaward side has been built up and partially embanked as a defence against the tides.'

'And the house?'

'While I was helping your father go through some old documents, we discovered that Saltmarsh House, which was built on a man-made mound, was used as a lighthouse in Tudor times.'

'That accounts for the tower. As a child I always thought the place looked like a lopsided castle.'

'It was a kind of castle in a way. It certainly became a stronghold. There were cannons to seaward, and at low tide the presence of dangerous quicksands helped to deter any land-based attacks.'

'You must have found the research interesting,' Quinn observed. Then, with no change of tone, he asked, 'How did you manage to get a job as my father's secretary?'

'You mean did I engineer it?'

'Did you?'

'No. I'd never heard of Henry Durville. He approached me.'

'Out of the blue?'

'Yes.'

Seeing Quinn's face register disbelief, she said flatly, 'I'd just left college and was looking for a job when Peter Carradine, my history tutor at Pentridge, got in touch with me.

'It seems that he and your father had been friends since their school days...'

'Go on.'

'When Henry's first stroke partially confined him to a wheelchair and he decided to research and record the Durville family history, he needed someone to help him. He went to see his old friend and ask if he knew anyone suitable, and Peter Carradine mentioned my name to him.'

Quinn still looked sceptical, and she said fiercely, 'You can check the truth of that if you want.'

'I might just do that.' Then he asked, a shade derisively, 'How did a history student metamorphose into a secretary?'

The spurt of anger dying, she answered flatly, 'I'd been warned that there weren't too many jobs available in my chosen field, so to be on the safe side I'd gone to special classes to learn shorthand and typing.'

'But it seems you utilized more potent skills.'

'I don't know what you mean,' she said stiffly.

'Oh, I think you do.'

What was the use of protesting her innocence? she thought bleakly. He was convinced she'd deliberately set out to catch his father, and there seemed to be no way to prove how wrong he was.

Sighing, she turned her head to look out of the window once more.

The rolling countryside had given way to flatter, lower-lying farmland, which turned to marsh as they got nearer to the coast.

Elizabeth was deep in thought, oblivious to her surroundings, when Quinn brought the car to a halt and suggested, 'It's getting quite late, so what about a post of lunch?'

Looking up, she saw that they were on one of the quiet back roads that skirted the little town of Saltmarsh and led down to the shore.

They had stopped outside the Ship, a black and white half-timbered inn, with bow-windows and a hanging sign showing a full-masted sailing clipper.

Shock made her heart lurch and her stomach start to churn. Finding her voice, she objected. 'Have we time to stop for lunch?'

'We need to eat somewhere—' Quinn's manner was deceptively casual '—and you said you liked this inn last time, if you remember?'

So stopping at the Ship was no accident. She shivered as the poignant memory of past happiness and delight mingled with alarm and dismay at finding herself here again in such very different circumstances.

Watching her face, he queried, 'Surely you haven't forgotten staying here?'

No, she hadn't forgotten. She and Quinn had been returning from London one evening, and had missed the tide. Unable to cross the causeway, they had been forced to stay at the inn.

He had calmly booked one room, and, though she was totally inexperienced, already fathoms-deep in love, and knowing he was the one man for her, she had made no demur.

When, hands clenched, she remained silent, he asked, 'Don't you remember the four-poster bed, and the grandfather clock that chimed so loudly in the middle of the night...?'

'No! No, I really don't remember.' She was lying through her teeth and he knew it.

'Not even the bedroom ceiling with its painted mermaids?' he asked wickedly, and watched the hot colour pour into her face.

When she was scarlet as a poppy, he slid from behind the wheel and came round to help her out.

'Another reason for choosing this place,' he went on, as he escorted her the few yards to the inn door, 'is that they display a tidetable. I can check when it's low tide.'

'What if we've already missed it?' The instant the question was out, she could have bitten her tongue.

He shrugged, and suggested, 'If we can't make it over to the island, we can stay here tonight and go across tomorrow.'

Panic stricken, she began, 'No, I can't stay overnight. Richard—'

'Is in Amsterdam,' Quinn jumped in smoothly, 'so he'll never know.'

She pulled herself together, and said, 'He often phones me when he's away.'

'Do you usually sit at home and wait?'

'Yes.'

Quinn muttered something half under his breath that Elizabeth didn't catch. But she saw that his mouth had tightened ominously, and she felt maliciously pleased that she'd managed to anger him.

The lounge, with its low, black-beamed ceiling and sloping floor, looked just the same. A cheerful log fire burnt in the wide fireplace, and the air was scented with applewood.

Apart from a marmalade kitten blinking sleepily at the flames, the place was empty.

Having settled Elizabeth at a table, Quinn dropped his jacket over the back of a chair and strolled over to study the tidetable.

Recalling what he'd said about staying the night, she asked anxiously, 'Is everything all right? Will we get across to the island?'

'There should be no problem at all,' he answered easily.

Just as he finished speaking, a genial-looking man with a neatly trimmed beard appeared behind the bar. Elizabeth gave a faint sigh of relief. To the best of her knowledge, she had never set eyes on him before.

'Not a very nice day,' he remarked cheerfully.

'No, the fog's never really cleared.' Quinn seemed prepared to discuss the weather while he glanced through a menu.

'Can't say I'm surprised,' the landlord said. 'It's forecast to linger for several days. Not that they always get it right, of course...'

After the exchange of pleasantries, and without consulting his companion, Quinn began to order their food.

Listening to him, she discovered he was ordering as near as possible the same things they'd eaten on their previous visit here, and realized that for some reason best known to himself he was trying to rattle her.

Well, she wouldn't let him succeed. She wouldn't give him that satisfaction.

When he returned carrying two glasses of bitter, her expression as untroubled as she could make it, she accepted one with a word of thanks.

As she sipped the clear, sharp brew, she found herself wondering what Richard would say if he could see her now.

He would probably be shocked.

Very conservative in some ways—she carefully avoided the term narrow-minded—and considering it infra dig, he never drank beer, and he had no idea she did. Though of course she *hadn't* since she'd known him...

The arrival of the starter broke into her rather confused thoughts. Staring at the dish of smoked Essex oysters and the thin fingers of toast, she remembered the last time when, seeing her hesitate, Quinn had asked quizzically, 'Don't you like smoked oysters?'

He had been twenty-seven then, good-looking and charismatic, already wealthy in his own right, and a knowledgeable man of the world.

She had been twenty-one, no great beauty, and, until she began to work for Henry Durville, a penniless history student.

Feeling very young and gauche, and at a grave disadvantage, she'd admitted, 'I don't know, I've never tried them.'

'Short of the adventurous spirit?'

'Short of money.'

Just for an instant his green eyes had looked very cold, then he'd raised an interested brow, inviting her confidence.

Even so, she'd kept it brief. 'For most of his adult life my father, who had a bad heart, was unable to work. We lived in a rented ground-floor flat and had a struggle to pay the bills, let alone buy luxuries.'

'And since?'

'Like most students I'm more familiar with baked beans than smoked oysters.'

His eyes amused now, he'd said, 'I think you'll find they're an improvement on baked beans. Why don't you go ahead and try one?'

Seeing he was waiting, she'd confessed awkwardly, 'I don't know what to *do* with them.'

'Then let me show you.' Quinn had put one of the smoked oysters on to a thin sliver of hot, buttered toast and fed it to her with his fingers.

His action had been intimate and strangely erotic, making her feel everything he'd wanted her to feel...

With a shiver, Elizabeth dragged her mind back to the

present and glanced up to find he was watching her, his gaze brilliant and intent.

He raised a dark brow. 'Can't remember what to do with them? Let me show you.' Putting one of the plum oysters on to a small piece of toast, he offered it to her.

She hadn't intended to take it, but like someone under a spell she opened her mouth, and saw his mocking smile.

Damn him! she thought bitterly, and fought the urge to spit it back in his handsome face.

'Enjoy that?' he asked, as she chewed and swallowed.

'Not really,' she answered flatly. 'I'm afraid my tastes have changed.'

'In *everything*?' he probed softly

A faint flush appearing along her cheekbones, she pretended not to have heard the loaded question.

He studied her, his dark eyes gleaming between thick, dark lashes. 'Refusing to say? Oh, well, it'll be fun finding out.'

She was suddenly hot and flustered, and her heart was racing, but telling herself firmly that he was just baiting her, she tried to hide her alarm.

As though he knew exactly what effect his words had had on her, he smiled a little, and with an air of satisfaction picked up his fork and began on his own share of oysters.

While the rest of the meal was served and eaten, he kept the conversation light, the topics general, making no further attempt to unsettle her.

Still she was relieved when their coffee cups were empty and they could start moving again. Now they'd got this far, all she wanted was to get the visit to Saltmarsh House over with as quickly as possible...

Once outside, Elizabeth found that the mist had closed in even more. The sky hung over the sea and the coastal plain like an inverted bowl of hazy pearl, and the still air felt raw and clammy.

She shivered, chilled by a combination of cold and nervous apprehension. 'We won't have to be too late starting back.'

'No,' he agreed, as he slid behind the wheel and started the car.

On either edge of the small town of Saltmarsh, the land was bleached and colourless, veined by numerous threads of silver from the many inlets and waterways that dissected it.

Though the coastline was in no way spectacular, it had its own kind of charm, and in the few months she had lived here Elizabeth had grown to love it.

'A fascinating coast in its own way.' Quinn echoed her thoughts.

'Yes,' she agreed. 'The Elizabethan topographer William Camden said of this county, "The ocean windeth itselfe into it."'

'Both poetic and accurate.'

After a few hundred yards the road that ran down to the sea petered out, and beyond the dark, gritty foreshore, and a stretch of lighter sand, the water looked calm as a mill-pond and pewter-grey.

At the far end of the half-mile-long causeway, partly obscured by mist, lay the familiar oval shape of Saltmarsh Island.

Stopping the car, Quinn rested his forearms on the wheel and stared across at the oblong bulk of the house and the squat round tower.

Watching him surreptitiously, she noted that his expression was curiously sombre, and wondered what he was thinking and feeling.

By his own admission, Saltmarsh House hadn't been home to him since he was a child, but it was bound to hold a lot of early memories, both happy and sad.

An early dusk had already started to close in and, to

Elizabeth, the old house looked unbearably lonely and desolate in the fading light.

Or was that only because she knew Henry was no longer there?

Perhaps she sighed aloud, because Quinn glanced at her before restarting the car.

They drove over the causeway—its edges marked at intervals by tall, thin white poles—past the large brick boathouse, and up a steep, paved incline to the house itself.

At one side of the substantially built terrace, there was an extensive garage block and a self-contained flat for the chauffeur, which had been added in Henry's lifetime.

As well as the family cars, the block had housed a supply of logs for the open fires, and a generator, though during the last twenty years all mod cons had been laid across to the island.

Quinn stopped the car in front of the garages, and, with the kind of consideration that had once made her feel loved and cherished, came round to open Elizabeth's door and help her out.

She had half expected the housekeeper to appear and welcome them, but even this close the house seemed deserted.

Uneasily, she remarked, 'I presume Mrs Wickstead knows you're coming?'

'I'm afraid Mrs Wickstead isn't here.'

'Isn't here?' Elizabeth felt a quick stab of alarm. 'But you said she still lived here.'

'So she does. It just happens that a short while ago she had to have an operation. She's gone to Harwich to stay with her sister until she's fully recovered.'

'Oh,' Elizabeth said blankly. Then she asked accusingly, 'Why didn't you tell me?'

'Does it make any difference?' he asked calmly.

It made all the difference.

'I just wish I'd known.' She sounded as agitated as she felt.

'You mean you wouldn't have come?'

'No, I wouldn't,' she burst out.

'Dear, dear,' he said mildly. 'Then it's just as well I forgot to mention it.'

'You didn't forget,' she accused. 'You kept it from me purposely.'

'Now why would I do a thing like that?'

She didn't dare begin to think.

CHAPTER FIVE

PULLING a key from his pocket, Quinn opened the heavy iron-studded door and ushered a reluctant Elizabeth into the panelled hall, which ran the entire width of the house.

It was poignantly familiar.

At either end, two long windows let in light which on sunny days made the black floorboards gleam. On the left was a wide stone fireplace, and in the centre an oak staircase curved upwards, with a specially fitted lift to take the wheelchair.

The air felt chill and, though the antique furniture still shone, the clean, fresh smell of beeswax polish that Elizabeth had always associated with the big old house was missing.

'If you'll excuse me a moment I'll turn up the central heating.' Quinn disappeared kitchenwards while she hovered, agitated and uncertain.

He was back quite quickly, remarking casually, 'It won't take too long for the place to warm up. In the meantime I'll get a fire going in the study.'

As he moved purposefully away, she followed him, protesting, 'But surely we won't be staying long enough to need a fire?'

'There are some of my father's private papers and his safe I still have to look through, so as we're going to be here for a while at least we might as well be cosy,' he pointed out reasonably.

The study, a combination of living room, office and library, was large and well-furnished, with a crimson carpet and rich velvet curtains. On the seaward side of the house, and with a huge, diamond-paned bow-window set in its two-foot-thick outer wall, it had been Henry's favourite room

There was a log fire already laid in the wide stone fireplace, and a box of matches on the mantelpiece, so it was the work of a moment for Quinn to stoop and set light to the kindling.

As it flamed and crackled, sending a shower of bright sparks up the chimney, he drew an armchair up to the blaze, and invited, 'Why don't you make yourself at home?'

Noting her reluctance to comply, her anxious glance at the door, he said humorously, 'Or perhaps you'd prefer to make a start? Your room is just as you left it, so if you want to look through the things I mentioned earlier…?'

Elizabeth shook her head. That part of her life was over and done with. She wanted no reminders. 'It isn't necessary. I don't intend to take any of them. If there's anything worth having it can go to Oxfam or some other charity.'

Trenchantly, he said, 'Then rather than hover like some restless spirit, may I suggest that you sit down and endeavour to possess your soul in patience while I get on with my part of the proceedings?'

Divesting himself of his jacket, he tossed it aside, and, crossing the room, took a seat behind Henry's large, imposing desk and switched on the lamp.

Sinking into the chair, and trying to ignore the pricking in her thumbs, she stared through the window-panes at the November dusk gathering over the sea.

Though she studiously avoided looking at Quinn, she was conscious of his every move. She heard him unlock and open one of the drawers, then the rustle of papers as he began to go through them.

She risked a quick glance. Seeing he was fully occupied, she began to watch him surreptitiously from beneath long, silky lashes.

His was the kind of tough, masculine beauty that had always made him a man's man and every woman's darling. But, though he must have been well aware that women often turned their heads to give him a second look, he had never shown any sign of personal vanity, nor had he made the slightest effort to encourage their interest.

He had once told her that he was a one-woman man, and, believing him implicitly, she had hoped and prayed that *she* might be that one special woman. That *she* might be the love of his life, the mother of his children...

Her heart full of pain and a bitter-sweet longing, Elizabeth studied his downbent face, the dark brows, a furrow of concentration between them, the bony nose, the heavy eyelids, and the sweep of dark lashes against his hard cheekbones.

It was a precious gift to be able to just sit and look at him; once it had seemed as necessary as breathing. Then, the thought of seeing him, of being with him, for the rest of her life had filled her with contentment and happiness.

But that was when she had foolishly imagined that he felt the same about her.

If only he *had* loved her. She felt a futile longing for what might have been, a bleak emptiness...

A lock of dark hair fell over his forehead. Raking it back with an impatient hand, Quinn glanced up and caught her eye.

Hastily she turned to look at the fire, and, slipping off her court shoes, stretched her stockinged feet to the comforting warmth.

The logs were well alight and blazing merrily now. Taking off her jacket, she leaned her head against the back of the chair and looked for pictures in the flames while she waited for him to finish his task.

Elizabeth was dreaming that Quinn was kissing her. His kiss was light, but sweeter than any wine, and joy flooded through her.

The dream was very real. She could feel his mouth moving softly, seductively against hers, asking for a response she was only too willing to give.

Her lips parted beneath the gentle pressure, and with a little inarticulate murmur of pleasure she reached out to put her arms around his neck.

As she touched him, she gave a stifled gasp and opened her eyes. Her dream lover was only too clearly flesh and blood.

He was leaning over her, a hand on either arm of her chair, trapping her there, his mouth just inches from hers.

Jerking her head aside, she cried, 'What are you doing?'

'Merely following the time-honoured way of waking a Sleeping Beauty.'

'I don't want you to kiss me,' she protested thickly.

'You did a moment ago.'

Unable to deny it, she stayed silent.

Straightening, he moved away and sat down in a chair that had been pulled up opposite, his eyes on her flushed face.

Still half dazed with sleep, she glanced around and discovered that the red velvet curtains had been drawn across the window, and the standard lamps switched on. Lit only by the twin pools of light and the leaping flames, the room looked snug and intimate.

Seeing the desk lamp was off, she asked, 'Have you finished working?'

'For the time being. I thought I'd have a break and come and sit by the fire.'

With a sudden insight, she knew as surely as if he'd admitted it that he'd been sitting watching her sleep. The knowledge disturbed her, making her feel exposed, vulnerable, and a shiver ran down her spine.

How long had he watched her? How long had she been asleep?

As though she'd spoken the question aloud, he said ironically, 'Despite having slept so well last night, you must have been tired. I've put logs on the fire more than once without you even stirring. In fact I'd begun to think you were settled for the evening.'

Trying, without much success, to tuck back the curly tendrils of silky dark hair that had escaped from her chignon, she asked, 'What time is it?'

She had no watch and there was no clock in the study. Henry had had an aversion to a clock ticking in the same room.

'Time for some tea,' Quinn answered casually. 'That's why I woke you. It's all ready.'

He got to his feet, and from the shadows behind her wheeled a trolley set with tea things. 'I'm afraid the milk from the freezer is still solid, so I made it Earl Grey.

'Perhaps you'd like to pour while I toast some muffins I found and defrosted? Luckily there was a new pack of butter left in the fridge—'

This cosy tête-à-tête wasn't at all what she'd been expecting, and it struck her as bizarre that two people with so much bitterness between them, so much misconception and downright animosity should be doing something as peaceful and commonplace as drinking tea and toasting muffins together.

Feeling as though she'd been caught up in some Alice-in-Wonderland scenario, she picked up the elegant silver teapot and filled two china cups while Quinn squatted on his haunches with a long-handled toasting fork.

The glow from the fire turned his strong-boned face into a bronze mask and made his eyes gleam as, his free arm resting on a muscular thigh, he toasted a pile of the light, spongy muffins.

When they were neatly stacked he began to butter them lavishly, querying, 'Are you hungry?'

Surprisingly, she was. 'Starving,' she admitted, and found herself smiling at him.

He smiled back, and it was as though they were friends.

Putting her share on to a plate, he suggested, 'Then start tucking in.'

When she'd finished the last bite, she licked her buttery fingers and said appreciatively, 'Mmm, they were absolutely delicious.'

'Not in the same class as caviare, of course?'

'But more my style.'

'Oh, I don't know,' he said lightly. 'You used to enjoy such delicacies.'

'I think I mentioned that my tastes have changed.' As soon as the words were out she regretted them, not wanting to go back to skirmishing, unwilling to destroy this feeling of closeness.

'So you did.' Softly, he added, 'But I still remember what you *used* to like.'

Suddenly, he was much too near. Her heart thudding like a trip-hammer, she held her breath as he reached out and rubbed a thumb across her bottom lip.

'A dribble of butter,' he explained, and smiled into her wide grey eyes.

When they dropped beneath the regard of his green ones, he resumed his seat, and asked, 'Tell me, Jo, do you remember when I took you out in the *Seawind*? We had caviare that day...'

'Please don't call me Jo,' she whispered.

'I called you darling then, and kissed you.'

She remembered it well. It had been one of those rare, golden days of Indian summer. The air had been balmy and the sea blue, and she had never felt so happy in her life—

'As I recall, you kissed me back.'

'I don't remember,' she denied unsteadily.

'After our picnic we found a sheltered cove and I spread a blanket on the sand. When I took you in my arms and began to make love to you, you responded with as much warmth and passion as any man could have wished for in his wildest dreams.

'In fact if the venue had been a little more private,' he added sardonically, 'I wouldn't have needed to arrange that trip to London and our overnight stay at the inn.'

Bitterly, she said, 'I might have known that was a planned seduction.'

'Hardly a seduction. As I recall you didn't need much enticing. Perhaps you should have held back a little. It would have made your pretence of being a virgin more believable.'

Lifting her chin, she said flatly, 'It wasn't a pretence.'

Hearing the unmistakable ring of truth in her voice, just for an instant Quinn looked shaken. 'I did wonder at the time, but it didn't tie in with stories of you coming out of Henry's room at all hours of the night.'

'Who told you that?' she demanded. 'Were you paying Mrs Wickstead to spy on me?'

Choosing to ignore her question, he asked, 'Were those stories true?'

'They were perfectly true,' she said evenly. 'Quite often, when Henry couldn't sleep, he'd give me a call and I'd go along and play chess with him.'

'Didn't it occur to you that visiting Henry's room at all sorts of strange hours was open to misinterpretation?'

'Perhaps because *I* knew it was perfectly innocent, I never gave it a thought. I'm afraid I was very naive in those days.'

'Wouldn't the word *calculating* be more accurate?'

In an instant the closeness was destroyed.

Cut to the heart, she said, 'No, it wouldn't.'

'Why don't you admit you were angling for my father until I came on the scene—?'

'I wasn't doing any such thing!'

Taking no notice of the interruption, he went on, 'But it didn't take you long to leave him flat when you figured that I was the better bet.'

'It wasn't like that at all.'

'You practically fell into my arms.'

Flushing, she muttered, 'I—I found you attractive.'

'Sexually?'

'Yes.'

'Money is sexy stuff,' he observed cynically.

'Money had nothing to do with it.'

'Then why did you go to bed with me for the asking?'

Her pride trampled into the dust, she cried, 'Because I was stupid enough to think I was in love with you.'

'Love at first sight?' he mocked. 'How very convenient.' Then he said bitingly, 'But if you're really trying to convince me it *wasn't* my money I'd be more likely to believe in *lust* at first sight.'

Fiercely, she said, 'Well, whatever it was, it didn't last.'

'Didn't it, Jo? I'd say the attraction is still there, as strong as ever. Would you like me to prove it to you?'

'No!' Agitation brought her to her feet. 'Isn't it time we were going?'

'Going where?'

'Back home, of course.' She reached for her shoes and pulled them on.

Lounging nonchalantly in his chair, he informed her, 'There's no point in our hurrying.'

'I've done as you asked and come here with you,' she said as evenly as possible. 'Now I'd like it if we could go.'

Patiently, he repeated, 'There's really no point in our hurrying.'

Maddened by his laid-back manner, she insisted, 'But if we don't get off soon it might to be too late.'

'I fear it's already too late.'

Unable to credit it, she began, 'Are you telling me—?'

'I'm telling you the causeway is already under water.'

'What time is it?' she demanded.

'Seven-thirty.'

'Seven-thirty!' She must have slept for several hours... 'Why didn't you wake me?'

'I did.'

'I mean sooner.' Quinn had looked at the tidetable, so he should have known they hadn't got too long.

'I'm afraid I lost track of time.'

The excuse was too glib, too facile.

Oh, why had she been fool enough to trust him? The tide must have been already on the turn when they'd driven across the causeway...

Catching at straws, she demanded, 'Are you *sure* we can't get back?'

'Take a look.'

Pulling on her jacket, she hurried across the hall, threw open the front door, and stepped outside.

Any hope she might have cherished died on the spot. Between the island and the hazy lights of the town was an unbroken expanse of foggy sea. The causeway had completely vanished.

Appearing at her side, Quinn said, 'I'm sure you agree that it's impassable?' His breath made puffs of white vapour on the chill air, as he went on calmly, 'So I'm afraid that means we're stranded here until morning.'

Feeling her shiver, he added, 'I suggest we go in out of the cold. There's no point standing here risking pneumonia.'

Stunned and unresisting, she allowed him to draw her inside, and close the door.

Leading the way back to the study, he helped her off with her jacket, and pushed her gently back into her chair.

Then, throwing another log on the fire, he resumed his own seat and remarked, 'As we won't be going anywhere, we might as well be comfortable.'

Something about the way he spoke jarred. He sounded well satisfied, quietly triumphant.

Abruptly she was convinced that being stranded here was no careless accident. The whole thing had been *deliberate*.

Unable to hide her anger and agitation, she choked, 'You *meant* this to happen. You *planned* it.'

'You must think I'm positively machiavellian,' he scoffed. 'Next, you'll be accusing me of giving you sleeping tablets.'

When she remained silent, he raised a dark brow. 'No? Well, that's a relief.'

In a rush, she charged, 'If I hadn't played into your hands by going to sleep, you'd have found some other way to keep us here until it was too late.'

'You seem very certain. Have you also decided what my motive is?'

'I don't know,' she admitted. 'Possibly to try and cause trouble.'

'You mean with regard to Beaumont? In my opinion you've already got enough problems in that direction.'

'And this is bound to add to them.'

'Well, if *you* don't tell him, *I* won't,' Quinn promised.

'It's not just that...' Biting her lip, she tried a softer approach. 'Please, Quinn, I really don't want to have to stay here...'

'You *must* be anxious to leave. That's the first time you've been able to bring yourself to use my name.'

Ignoring the derision, she persisted, 'Can't we go over by boat? It isn't *too* foggy.'

'You're suggesting we stay overnight at the Ship and come back for the car in the morning?'

'Yes,' she said eagerly. Anything was better than being trapped here with him in complete isolation.

But he was shaking his head with mock regret. 'I'm afraid that's not possible. You see, there aren't any boats here any longer. It seems Henry decided not to bother keeping them.'

Watching all her new-found hope change to despair, he said chidingly, 'There's no need to look quite so desperate. After all, I am your husband.'

He was so tough, so sure of himself, so arrogant.

'But you're not! At least...'

'Only in the eyes of the law?' he finished for her. 'Well, if you *do* want to share my bed, at least it will be legal.'

'I *don't* want to share your bed,' she said jerkily. 'I came here so you'd agree to an annulment, not to complicate matters further.'

'Well, if you're just worrying about *complicating* things—'

'I'm not just worrying about complicating things.' Even as she denied it, she knew this confrontation was going to develop into a running battle, with her doing the running.

'That's what it sounds like.'

'Believe me, I have no desire to sleep with you,' she told him, and was aware that she lied. Clenching her teeth, she added, 'I've promised to marry Richard, and I'd hate anything to spoil that.'

'Well, if it's just a rich husband you want, may I point out that you already have one?'

'I don't just want a rich husband. I want Richard. I *love* him.'

'Now why do I get the feeling that when you say you love Beaumont you're trying to convince yourself as well as me?'

'As it's not true, I really can't imagine.'

'Tell me, Jo, is he a good lover?'

'That's nothing to do with you,' she snapped.

'If you're comparing the two of us it's a relevant question.'

'I'm not comparing the two of you!'

'Is that because you don't want to? Or because you can't?'

'I don't want to.'

'Why not? I'd have thought it would give you a great deal of satisfaction to compare the two of us and find me wanting... When you're so strangely reticent it makes me wonder if you *have* slept with him?'

At the end of her tether, she cried, 'All right, I *haven't*, if that makes you feel any better?'

'No wonder the poor devil looked so frustrated,' Quinn observed with a grin. Then he asked swiftly, 'Why not?'

'Perhaps I'm old-fashioned enough to want a ring on my finger first,' she retorted sweetly.

He laughed, white teeth gleaming, before reminding her, 'You weren't with me.'

'As I've already said, I was naïve and foolish then. I'm wiser now.'

'You must also be frustrated? Or perhaps you have a lover on the side?'

'Sorry to disappoint you.'

'How many have there been since me?'

'Dozens,' she said airily.

Suddenly, he was on his feet and hauling her out of her chair. 'I want the truth.'

'I thought you wanted something more exciting.'

His fingers biting into the soft flesh of her upper arms through the thin silk of her blouse, he shook her slightly. 'How many?'

'None,' she admitted wearily.

Some powerful emotion flitted across his face, but before she could decipher it it was gone. His expression became inscrutable, the splendid bone structure a mask to hide his thoughts.

'I find that surprising,' he said after a moment, and, releasing her, stepped back to allow her to resume her seat again. 'You're a very passionate woman.'

Leaning a shoulder against the stone mantelpiece, he stood looking down at her consideringly. 'I remember the first time I made love to you, you went up like straw—and I don't believe you were faking it—'

'I'd rather not talk about the past,' she broke in, her voice ragged.

'Well, as we don't seem to have any future, at least not together, the past is all we have to talk about— Unless you'd like to speculate on how good your chances are of being happy with Beaumont...'

She stopped running and turned, at bay. 'A great deal better than my chances of being happy with you! At least he loves me. You didn't even *like* me. You felt nothing for me...'

'Ah, but I did. Despite knowing exactly what you were up to, I was infatuated from the word go. And though I despised myself for wanting a worthless little gold-digger I felt furiously jealous and possessive every time you so much as smiled at my father.'

Though he'd said *did*, and *was*, and *infatuated*, in an odd sort of way, knowing he'd once felt *something* for her, even against his will, was a comfort.

She'd got so used to believing he'd felt nothing but dislike and disapprobation, and the kind of sexual desire any red-blooded male might have felt for any nubile female...

'Tel me, Jo—' his slightly husky voice broke into her thoughts '—if I hadn't put in an appearance, would you have married him?'

'What makes you think he'd have asked me?'

'He was in love with you. Otherwise why would he have left you half his estate?'

'Henry cared about me, but that isn't the same thing at all. And I don't know *why* he left me half his estate. In the circumstances I wish to God he hadn't.'

Cynically, Quinn suggested, 'I suppose from your point of view it would have been better if I'd stayed in Boston and you'd simply become a rich widow?'

'I wouldn't have married him. There was no question of it.'

'You told me you were fond of him.'

'I was. But I didn't love him in that way. I looked on him more as a father.'

'Don't you mean a sugar daddy?'

'He didn't give me any gifts, if that's what you're implying.'

Quinn straightened. 'Sure?'

'Quite sure. Apart from the locket I had for my twenty-first birthday. And you know about that. You saw me wearing it.'

The chased silver locket, bought at Covent Garden on one of the trips she and Henry had made to London, had been comparatively cheap. Something she'd paused to look at on one of the stalls. Seeing she'd taken a fancy for it, he'd insisted on getting it for her birthday, which happened to be that very day.

'Yes, I know about the locket,' Quinn said a shade impatiently, 'but what about the earrings?'

'Earrings?' she echoed blankly. 'What earrings?'

Quinn pulled a soft leather wallet from his jacket pocket and, removing something from it, held out his hand. Lying in his palm were the mermaid earrings he'd taken from her lobes the previous night.

So much had happened that she'd forgotten all about them.

Watching her face, he remarked, 'Exquisite, aren't they? The workmanship is exceptionally fine.'

'I think so,' she agreed. 'But what have they to do with Henry?'

Ignoring the question, Quinn said carefully, 'I never saw you wearing *them* when we first knew each other.'

'Maybe that's because I didn't have them then.'

'And maybe it's because you were hiding them.'

'Hiding them? Why on earth should I be hiding them?'

'Because you didn't want me to know Henry had given them to you.'

'Henry didn't give them to me.'

'So you're denying it?'

'I most certainly am!'

'Then where did you get them? You told me your family was poor, and they aren't the kind of baubles you could pick up on a market stall.'

Infuriated by his arrogance, she said hotly, 'Where I got them from is none of your business! Now can I please have them back?'

'I think not.' Ignoring her gasp of outrage, he returned them to his wallet. 'I need to do some checking. If Henry didn't give them to you—'

'He *didn't*,' she broke in angrily.

'And you won't tell me where they came from, then I can only presume that you took them.'

Agitation brought her to her feet. 'Took them? You mean *stole* them? How dare you?' she choked furiously. 'You've accused me of being a heartless gold-digger, of trying to seduce your father, of marrying you for your money, and now you've got the nerve to suggest I'm a thief!'

'If I'm wrong about you, I'll apologize,' he said evenly.

'But I don't believe any apologies will be necessary. I know only too well what kind of woman you are.'

'You may think you know, but you're quite wrong. I'm *none* of the things you've charged me with being. And I am *certainly* not a thief!'

'Then Henry did give them to you?' he pressed.

'I've already told you he *didn't*...'

Just as she finished speaking one of the burning logs rolled into the hearth with a crash, sending a shower of red hot sparks on to the carpet.

Quinn ground them out with the toe of his shoe, before reaching for the tongs to replace the log.

Unable to stand any more, in a stifled voice Elizabeth said, 'I'm going to bed.' Jumping to her feet, she started for the door.

'May I suggest you wait just a moment?' Something about the way Quinn spoke stopped her in her tracks. 'You'll probably need this.'

Turning, she saw him reach behind the desk and produce a small overnight case she recognized as belonging to her.

Taken aback, she demanded, 'Where did you get that?'

'I brought it in from the trunk of the car when you were asleep.'

Seeing her soft lips tighten, he said innocently, 'Oh, you mean before that? I found it in your wardrobe. While you were in the bathroom this morning I took the opportunity to pack a few things, just in case we were forced to stay the night.'

His sheer effrontery took her breath away.

'So you *did* plan the whole thing!'

'I thought you'd already decided that?'

'And this confirms it! But why?'

'Earlier, if I remember rightly, you supplied your own answer.'

'But you promised you wouldn't tell Richard.'

'Nor will I. Whatever happens.'

Her voice shrill with alarm, she demanded, 'What do you mean, *whatever happens*?'

He shrugged. 'Just that. Now, if you'd like a hot drink before you go, I've found a tin of drinking chocolate...'

'No, I wouldn't, thank you.'

'Sure? It might help you sleep.'

'I won't need any help,' she said tightly.

'Then I'll say pleasant dreams.'

Suddenly he was much too close. Taking her unawares, his hands came up to frame her face, and, his glance lingering with insolent sensuality on her mouth, he suggested, 'I thought just a goodnight kiss for old times' sake?'

'No!' Her exclamation held both anger and alarm.

'Why so cautious? Which of us are you afraid to trust, I wonder? Me or yourself?'

Before she could answer, or make any further protest, he bent his dark head and his mouth claimed hers in a kiss that started as an arrogant statement of male domination, but after a moment gentled to one of sweet seduction.

When her lips parted helplessly beneath the sensuous demand of his, his arms went around her and held her close.

Head spinning, she melted against him, while he kissed her as though he was starving for her, as though he'd waited years for this moment.

Nothing in the world existed beyond this man's arms and this man's hungry mouth, and she was almost lost, when deep in her subconscious a warning bell rang.

Managing to find the strength of mind from somewhere, she tore herself free, and, the back of one hand pressed to her mouth, her grey eyes dazed and darkened to charcoal, stood swaying as if she were intoxicated.

Quinn, though looking hardly less dazed, and breathing as if he'd been running, was the first to recover.

Huskily, he said, 'For a goodnight kiss, that engendered

a fair bit of heat. So perhaps you were right to be cautious— Unless you've changed your mind about spending the night in my arms?'

Shaken to the core by the stark longing she could read on his face, she managed a hoarse, 'No, I haven't,' and turned to the door.

'Don't forget your night things,' he reminded her. Then he said softly, 'If you *do* change your mind I'll be waiting.'

Grabbing both the case and her shoulder-bag, shocked and frightened by the closeness of her escape, Elizabeth fled on legs that were barely able to support her.

When she reached her room she put her things on a low chest and sank on to the bed, trembling in every limb. There was a lock on the door, but she knew instinctively that it wouldn't be necessary to use it. No matter how much Quinn wanted her, he wouldn't come to her; she was certain of that. He would wait for her to go to him.

And she was tempted as she'd never been tempted in her life before—

How was it possible to feel so much for a man who, though he might still want her, in the purely physical sense of the word, thought so ill of her?

If only he would agree to a quick annulment— Once she was safely married to Richard she would have security and a contented family life. If it was no grand passion, all the better. She had seen where passion could lead.

The last encounter with Quinn had almost wrecked her life. It had taken years to recover some pride and self-respect, and find a kind of emotional stability.

No, she couldn't, *wouldn't* get involved with him again; it would be the utmost folly.

Yet the memory of his hunger was like a giant fist squeezing her heart, so that her chest was filled with pain and her resolution faltered.

But she mustn't let it.

Head bent, hands clenched tightly together, she fought a silent battle.

And won.

CHAPTER SIX

LIFTING her chin, she looked around the large, white-walled room, with its low, beamed ceiling, black oak floorboards, and few pieces of antique furniture. She had always loved its simplicity, and the view across the water to the old town.

As Quinn had said, it was pretty much as she'd left it. The bed was covered by her favourite hand-made patchwork quilt, and there were soft peach towels in the modern, well-appointed bathroom—as though she'd been expected back.

It gave her the strangest feeling.

Some of her clothes still hung in the wardrobe, and a few personal possessions were scattered about. A small travel clock, a pair of sunglasses, a college pop-concert programme, and on the bow-fronted chest of drawers, in a plain wooden frame, a snapshot of herself and Henry.

Picking it up, she stared at it, and felt all the old fondness come flooding back.

Though Quinn's build was similar, in every other respect Henry had been more like his younger son, both men having a snub nose and a slight gap between the top two front teeth.

He had been kind and considerate, a truly *nice* man, with a slow smile and a dry sense of humour. The kind of man who, though over six feet tall and well-built, wouldn't have hurt a fly.

His silver hair had been thick and springy, and a boyish, unlined face and a quiet love of life had made him seem appreciably younger than his years.

The photograph had been taken on a calm, sunny day in

late summer. Wearing a simple cotton dress and sandals, her hair gathered up in a pony-tail, she looked girlish and carefree.

Henry, dressed in casual trousers and a short-sleeved shirt, had been out of his chair for his daily walk along the terrace. His walking stick was in one hand, and his free arm was around her shoulders for additional support.

He'd made some joke about being able to beat any wounded snail they might encounter, and, her head slightly turned, she had been laughing up at him just as Piery had appeared with his camera.

The whole thing had been happy and perfectly innocuous, but looking at it now she could see how it might possibly be misinterpreted.

How Quinn would *certainly* misinterpret it.

Sighing, she replaced it on the chest of drawers.

Thoughts of Quinn crowding once more into her mind, she opened her case to find her night things and get ready for bed.

He had been very thorough. As well as a nightdress and negligée—her best ivory satin ones, she noted wryly—he'd included two sets of undies, some flat-heeled shoes, two pairs of tights, a fine woollen dress, a skirt and jumper, and her spare toilet bag.

Though alarmed and angry that, for some twisted motive of his own, he'd deliberately placed her in this predicament, she could only marvel at his care and concern for her comfort.

Some macho men would never have given it a moment's consideration, she thought, as she stepped into the shower; or, if they had, would probably have dismissed it as spoiling their image.

But Quinn had always been something of an enigma. He could be both tough and tender, harsh and soft, sweet and bitter, caring and callous.

She had never known which was the real Quinn. But she had loved him anyway. Loved him with a depth and passion that had surprised even herself.

An enduring passion. A passion she had done her best to stifle, but which had flared into life the moment she saw him again. A passion which she now knew would be almost impossible to kill...

So how could she even *think* of marrying Richard?

The answer was, she couldn't. While she still felt this way about her first husband, there was no way she could marry anyone else.

Except that Quinn *wasn't* her husband...

And if she *had* weakened and shared his bed, though it would have been wonderful, she would have bitterly regretted it in the morning. Because nothing could come of a warped relationship like theirs.

Her heart like lead, she finished drying herself, cleaned her teeth, brushed out her long black hair, and, climbing into bed, turned out the light.

Lying with closed eyes, she did her best to relax, but try as she might she was unable to halt the thoughts that still ricocheted through her mind.

What must have been an hour or more later she was still wide awake, and weary of tossing and turning. The hot chocolate that she had refused now seemed like a good idea, not to say a necessity.

Getting out of bed, Elizabeth felt for her negligée and pulled it on. Opening her door, she switched on the landing light, and was blinking a little in the sudden brightness before second thoughts made her pause.

She had no idea which room Quinn was using, but if he wasn't asleep any crack of light under his door might disturb him.

Hurriedly she switched it off and, in darkness, made her way down the familiar stairs.

Crossing the hall, where the long windows made slightly lighter rectangles and her bare feet squeaked on the polished floorboards, she padded into the kitchen.

Turning on the strip lighting over the units, she put water in the kettle and looked in the cupboard for the drinking chocolate. She was just reaching for a mug when a movement, rather than a sound, made her realize she was no longer alone.

She spun round with a gasp to find a tall, dark shape was filling the shadowy doorway.

'I see you've changed your mind,' Quinn commented, adding ironically, 'About the drink, I mean.'

'You startled me,' she muttered. Then, her dismay evident, she asked, 'How did you know I was here?'

'I heard you cross the hall.'

He came towards her, and as he got within the range of the lights she could see he was still fully dressed, and it was obvious he hadn't been to bed at all.

His eyes travelling appreciatively over her slender, satin-robed figure, from the dark silky hair tumbled around her shoulders to her bare feet, he remarked, 'I take it you couldn't sleep after all?'

Ignoring the taunt, she demanded, 'Why have you followed me?'

'I was considering having a drink myself, so I thought it would be nice for us to have it together by the fire.'

She shook her head. 'I was intending to take mine back with me.'

'Well, we can have it in bed if you prefer.'

Struggling to retain her calm, refusing to let him ruffle her, she said, 'That wasn't what I meant, and you know it.'

'Then in front of the fire it is.'

The kettle boiled, and while Elizabeth hovered uncomfortably, wishing she'd stayed safely in her room, he filled a couple of mugs, and spooned in the drinking chocolate.

'Not exactly cordon bleu standard,' he remarked, as he
stirred the creamy concoction, 'but a few digestive biscuits
should help.'

After putting the mugs and the unopened packet of biscuits on a small round tray, he led the way back to the
study, leaving her to follow helplessly.

Feeling at a disadvantage because he was dressed and
she wasn't, Elizabeth tightened the belt of her robe and took
the seat she'd vacated earlier.

The logs in the grate were still blazing cheerfully, and a
pile of documents on the coffee table suggested Quinn had
been working by the fire.

Pushing the papers aside, he put the tray down and
passed her one of the mugs, before tearing open the packet
and offering her a biscuit.

When she shook her head, he helped himself to one before remarking casually, 'I've been taking another look at
Henry's will. At the date, to be precise. It occurred to me,
somewhat belatedly, that when it was made might have
some relevance...'

In the past, Elizabeth had noticed that Quinn's thoughts
often echoed her own, as if, as he'd remarked previously,
they were mentally close, on the same wavelength.

While she'd been trying to sleep, her own thoughts had
strayed to the will, and it had occurred to her to wonder
when it was dated...

But Quinn was continuing. 'If it had been made early
on, it would seem to prove that Henry loved you in the
way I'd always thought.

'Yet if that was the case, surely he would have altered
it when you ran off and married me. God knows he was
angry enough.'

'He wasn't angry when I saw him.' She spoke impul-
sively, without thinking.

'Say that again,' Quinn demanded sharply.

In the past she had found him formidable, and with that cold, narrow-eyed look he could still intimidate her. But this time, determined not to let him, she repeated firmly, 'Henry wasn't angry when I saw him.'

'Oh? And when was that?'

'When I went to break the news to him that I was going to marry you, and say goodbye.' Flushing a little, she added, 'I know you wanted to keep it a secret, but I couldn't just walk out without a word.'

'And you say he wasn't angry?'

'Quite the opposite. He was startled by the suddenness, but when he asked me if I...'

Watching her closely, Quinn probed, 'What did he ask?'

'If I loved you,' she said, her voice impeded.

'And what did you say?'

'I told him I did, and he looked delighted. He said in that dry way of his, "I've noticed you and Quinn couldn't keep your eyes off each other... Most people would call that folie à deux—utter madness for two people to fall in love so quickly—but I can't agree."'

'He went on to say he would miss me when I went to the States. But I could swear he was happy about it.'

Quinn looked shaken.

'I can't understand why he was so angry with you,' she added helplessly.

'Oh, I can,' Quinn said slowly. 'If what you say is true.'

'It is.'

Watching his hard profile, Elizabeth wondered what he was thinking, whether or not he believed her. There was a long silence while, his face curiously set and sombre, he stared into the fire.

A log burnt through and, with a rustle, settled into glowing greyish-white ash.

Quinn stirred, and turned his head to look at her. His voice curiously flat, he admitted, 'It was after you'd vanished into thin air, and he'd discovered that I'd married you for all the wrong reasons. He blamed me for driving you away.

'He made the will shortly after that... I'm sure he never gave up hope of finding you.'

Elizabeth's eyes filled with tears. Henry was the only one who had been genuinely fond of her, who had believed in her and trusted her.

She felt deeply ashamed that all she'd cared about was herself, her own misery, her own pain and loss. If only she'd got in touch with him before it was too late...

Seeing her emotion, Quinn reached out and put a hand over hers. That gesture of compassion was her undoing. All at once the tears overflowed and spilled down her cheeks. One dropped on to the back of Quinn's hand. Mortified, she clumsily wiped it away.

He muttered something under his breath, and a moment later he was on his feet and pulling her into his arms.

All the tension of the last twenty-four hours suddenly finding release, she began to sob unrestrainedly. Weeping not only for Henry, but for the whole sorry mess, and for what might have been.

When she'd learned of Quinn's perfidy, she'd been too frozen for tears, and in all the long years that followed she hadn't once cried. Now it was as if the floodgates had opened and she was unable to stop.

Gathering her to him with a tenderness that almost managed to convince her he really did care, Quinn cradled her head against his chest and held her, his mouth muffled against her scented hair.

When she was all cried out, he lifted her blotched face and wiped away the rest of her tears with his thumbs, before holding her close once more.

Completely drained, with no thought beyond that moment, she accepted the solace he offered, leaning against his strength, as if she'd come home.

One hand smoothing up and down her spine in an age-old gesture of comfort, he began to kiss her forehead, her damp cheeks, her closed eyelids, and finally her lips.

His mouth moving against hers sparked off a passionate response that she had neither the strength nor the will to fight. Her arms went around his neck and she was lost.

When he picked her up in his arms and carried her upstairs to his bedroom, she made not the slightest protest.

Elizabeth stirred and floated to the surface with a sense of euphoria, a singing gladness that filled her heart and mind and clung to her entire being, as tenuous yet strong as a golden cobweb.

Keeping her eyes closed, she lay quite still, savouring this extraordinary feeling of happiness, knowing she'd never felt such pleasure since Quinn had—

Quinn.

Memories of the previous night flooded into her mind and took her breath away. He had laid her down on his bed and made love to her with a hot, hungry passion that had sent them both up in flames and had taken most of the night to expend.

Then, some time before dawn, he had wakened her with a kiss and made love to her again, this time with a slow, leisurely enjoyment that had brought the most exquisite delight she had ever known.

The remembrance made a shiver run through her.

'Cold?'

Her eyes flew open.

Quinn was lying propped on one elbow, looking down at her sleep-flushed face and the black silky hair spread over the white pillow. Kissing her lightly, he repeated, 'Cold?'

'No.' It was just a whisper.

In the half-light she could see his hair was a little mussed, his green eyes were clear and bright, and a dark stubble adorned his chin.

She had never expected to see him like that again, and her heart seemed to do a back-flip.

He brushed some tendrils of hair away from her cheeks and smiled at her, his face holding a rare warmth and tenderness. 'I hope you enjoyed your wedding night?'

Watching her flush deepen, he asked, 'Do you realize that apart from the night we spent together at the Ship this is the only time we've wakened in the same bed?'

His hand, a hand that could be both cruelly strong and heartbreakingly tender, moved to cup and fondle a creamy breast. He added, 'I've dreamt about this ever since you ran away.' Then he exclaimed with a sudden bitterness, 'What a waste of five years! We could have had so much, if you hadn't left me.'

She brushed his hand aside and sat up, all her shining happiness draining away like water down a plughole. 'After finding out that you only married me to protect your father, what else was I to do?'

Pushing himself upright, he said carefully, 'You still haven't told me *how* you found out.'

'It isn't important.'

'It is to me,' he told her shortly. 'Though it didn't seem to make sense, I couldn't help but wonder if my father had had something to do with it. But if what you told me earlier was true...'

'It *was* true, and Henry had nothing to do with it.'

'Then *how*?'

She swallowed. 'I don't see any point in keeping going over the same ground. It doesn't matter how I found out. What does matter is that it was the truth.'

'Only partly. There were other considerations.'

'I know.' Then, echoing Quinn's bitterness, she said, 'Against your will, and in spite of everything, you still wanted me.'

'It was rather more than mere *wanting*. You were like a fever in my blood. You still are. When you ran out on me I hoped I'd be cured, but I soon found I wasn't. In fact if anything it got worse.

'We were married, yet not married... I knew I'd never be free of that fever until I'd made you my wife in reality as well as on paper.'

'So that was the unfinished business you mentioned?' Without waiting for an answer, she rushed on, 'Well, now it's finished—'

'Ah, but I'm not so sure it is.'

Taking no notice of the interruption, she added doggedly, 'I'd like my freedom.'

'If you're talking about an annulment, I'm afraid it's too late,' he pointed out with satisfaction.

'Then it will have to be a divorce.'

'You're not still hoping to marry Beaumont?' Quinn's whole body was taut, his voice cold as a winter sea.

'No.'

Almost imperceptibly, he relaxed. 'When did you change your mind? Was it *before* or *after*?'

Flushing a little, she asked, 'What difference does it make?'

'Quite a lot.'

'Very well, it was *before*.' Her voice full of self-contempt, she added, 'Perhaps if I'd wanted to marry him badly enough it would have saved me making the same mistake twice.'

'So you still regard it as a mistake?'

'What else can I regard it as? Oh, why did you have to come back into my life? I could have been happy with Richard.'

His face showing his scepticism, Quinn asked, 'What could he have given you that I couldn't?'

'Apart from love, you mean?'

'Is love so important to you?'

Lifting her chin, she admitted, 'Yes, it is!'

'As you probably know, anybody can *say* they love someone.'

Ignoring the gibe, she said hardily, 'I believe he *meant* it. But, even more important, with him I would have had my self-respect...'

Seeing Quinn's mouth tighten, she went on, 'Thinking so little of me, I'm surprised you still wanted me. In five years you must have come across plenty of women who were beyond reproach.'

'Unfortunately, I found no other woman would do.'

'Surely you're not trying to tell me you've been celibate for all that time?' she scoffed.

'No, I'm not,' he said evenly. 'What I am trying to tell you is that, apart from answering a basic need, no other woman has been of the slightest importance to me. I have taken a partner from time to time, but never a lover.'

She believed him, and, though she knew it was absurd, felt a surge of relief and gladness.

He picked it up at once. 'You seem pleased.'

'Why should I be pleased?' She was instantly on the defensive. 'I really don't care how many lovers you've had.'

Touching her nose with a fingertip, he commented, 'If you're not careful it'll grow.'

'I—I don't know what you mean,' she stammered.

'I mean you're lying. I believe you do care.'

Biting her lip, she looked away.

Studying her half-averted face—the pure bone structure, the lovely curve of her cheek, the winged brow—he went on, 'I find it hard to believe you ever loved me, but after the way you responded to me last night I'm convinced of one thing. You have the same kind of fever in your blood that I do, and five years spent apart hasn't managed to cure it.'

He reached out to take her chin and turn her face to his. 'That being the case, I suggest we stay together until the fever's run its course and we can both be free. Then I'll give you a quick, easy divorce.'

Hardly able to breathe for the pain his words caused, she jerked her head away and cried hoarsely, 'I wouldn't stay with you if my life depended on it.'

Looking as though her words were rocks she'd hit him with, he said slowly, 'I thought after last night—'

'Last night was a terrible mistake. It should never have happened.'

'But it *did* happen, and it proved a lot.'

'All it proved was that I'm the world's worst fool.'

As he looked about to interrupt, she rushed on, 'I must have been out of my mind to sleep with a man who thinks I'm nothing but a mercenary bitch, and possibly even a thief.'

Pushing aside the duvet, she was about to get out of bed, when Quinn caught her arm and kept her there. 'Where were you thinking of going?'

'I'm leaving. Now.'

Shaking his head, he said with mock regret, 'I'm afraid not.'

'I'm leaving,' she reiterated stubbornly. 'If you won't take me, I'll walk across.'

'You'll do no such thing. A mercenary bitch you may be, but I've no intention of letting you run out on me for a second time.'

'You can't make me stay.'

'Don't bet on it.' He gripped her shoulders. 'Look, Jo, don't let's—'

'Take your hands off me,' she interrupted fiercely.

'Leave me alone. I never want to see you again.' She began to struggle frantically, hitting out in a panic when he refused to release her.

Fending off her blows, he used the weight of his body to hold her down while he captured her wrists and, transferring them to one hand, pinned them above her head.

'I hate you,' she spat at him. 'I can't bear you to touch me.'

He stiffened, danger in every taut line of his body, and when he looked at her she saw smouldering fury in the green eyes.

'That's tough,' he said softy, 'because while you're still my wife and I still want you I'm going to touch you whenever I choose.'

'Rape me, you mean,' she said thickly.

'No, that isn't what I mean. I've never been remotely tempted to take a woman against her will, and I won't be starting now...'

He bent his head and kissed her averted cheek, his lips brushing light as thistledown over the flawless skin, before tracing a path to beneath her ear.

'You see, my love, it won't be necessary.'

The endearment caught her off guard, and she shivered as his mouth moved to caress the sensitive place where her neck and shoulder met.

While he continued to kiss her, his mouth sending erotic messages to every nerve-ending in her body, he whispered, 'You're so beautiful... Truly my pleasure, my passion, my pain... I've waited so long to have you in my arms, in my bed...wanted you more than I imagined it was possible to want any woman...'

She had half expected an onslaught, but instead he was showing her his weakness, his need, how seductive his desire could be.

Somehow she managed, 'I don't want you.'

He smiled against her skin. 'I don't believe you. I don't know what kind of hunger is strong enough to bind us together after so many years apart, but whatever it is you feel it too...'

His lips travelled down over the soft curve of her breast, his tongue-tip circling and laving the rosy nipple, until it firmed beneath his touch.

Then his mouth closed over it, causing such exquisite pleasure that it was almost pain. While he suckled sweetly, his hand moved to fondle the curve of her hip, the flat stomach, the long smooth line of her thigh.

She made a sound in her throat, and he lifted his head and kissed her mouth, which was still tightly closed. Releasing her hands, he cupped her face, and between little plucking kisses whispered against her lips, 'Open your mouth for me... You know you want to.'

If he'd been rough she might have withstood the siege, but he was tormentingly tender, using every last ounce of his skill and knowledge to make her want him.

Her lips parted on a sigh, and he kissed her by right of conquest.

Signifying her surrender, she put her arms around his neck and drew him down to her. When he settled himself into the cradle of her hips, her body welcomed his as part of itself.

It seemed to be a moment of supreme fulfilment, two separate bodies melded into a single entity and sharing the purest, most intimate of all human joys.

Only a small section of her mind stood apart, unhappy and dissenting, knowing there could be no greater humiliation than to love a man who not only despised her, but despised himself for wanting her.

When it was over, and their heartbeats and breathing had returned to normal, Quinn lifted himself away, leaving her feeling suddenly cold and bereft.

Watching him, she saw there was a glow about him that could have been happiness, but which was almost certainly triumph.

He reached out a long arm and, gathering her close, settled her head on his shoulder and kissed her. Sounding, to Elizabeth's ears, unbearably smug and self-satisfied, he said, 'Perhaps now we can stop all this talk of leaving, and make some plans for our future.

'During this last year I've had to spend so much time on Wall Street that I was considering either handing that side of the business over to someone else or moving to New York.

'When you've had a chance to see both Boston and the Big Apple, and find which you prefer, it will be easier to make a decision...'

So he imagined he'd won not just the battle, but the war.

Well, he was wrong!

Feeling as though a silken net was closing around her, Elizabeth moved restively. Meeting Quinn's questioning glance, she said the first thing that came into her head. 'What time is it?'

He looked at his watch. 'Almost one-thirty.'

'One-thirty!' she exclaimed in disbelief.

Laughing, he said, 'Well, we did have a busy night, and in this kind of weather—' he indicated the window, where a grey, patchy fog partially obscured the view '—it doesn't really matter if we stay in bed all afternoon.'

'It does to me.' She spoke without thinking. Then, noting his change of expression, she continued hastily, 'I'm ready for something to eat.'

His long fingers caressing her cheek and jaw, he suggested, 'Well, as we've five years to make up for and this is the start of our honeymoon, if you want to stay where you are, I'll raid the store cupboard and we'll have lunch in bed.'

Keeping her voice as steady as possible, she said, 'I'd prefer to get up. As I mentioned before, I don't like eating in bed.'

'Very well,' he agreed with obvious reluctance, and gave her a light kiss.

Trying not to look as if she was running away, she got out of bed, and, aware that his eyes were on her, hurriedly pulled on her satin negligée.

She was heading for the door when, with a teasing sidelong smile, he enquired, 'I don't suppose you'd care to share a shower?'

'No, I wouldn't, thank you,' she answered primly, and bolted.

Returning to her own room, she showered and dressed at record speed. The sooner they had eaten and were off the island, the better it would suit her. Every minute spent in Quinn's company was fraught with temptation, and if she weakened once more...

But she mustn't.

If she went back to him, knowing just what he thought of her would nag at her day and night and destroy any chance of happiness. And when his fever had run its course, and he tired of her, the final parting would be that much harder to bear.

Wearing her oatmeal jumper and donkey-brown skirt, her hair loose around her shoulders, she pushed the rest of her things back in the case and went down to the kitchen.

Switching on the lights to alleviate the November gloom, she opened the doors of the store cupboard. A hasty search produced tinned sausages, ham and tomatoes, all of which she fried while a small loaf from the freezer defrosted.

A pot of coffee was ready, and she was just dishing up the makeshift lunch, when Quinn appeared wearing well-cut grey trousers and a black polo shirt.

'Mmm...that smells good.' Brushing her hair aside, he

dropped a light kiss on her nape before taking a seat at the kitchen table.

He ate with a healthy appetite while, wondering how best to handle the situation when they got back to London, Elizabeth merely picked at hers.

'Something wrong?' His question made her jump.

'No.' Aware she sounded flustered, she added, 'Of course not.'

'You seem very *distraite*. It makes me wonder if you're planning something...'

CHAPTER SEVEN

'I was thinking.'

He pursed his lips. 'Not particularly happy thoughts, judging by the look on your face.'

Cursing herself, knowing she must allay his suspicions, Elizabeth said with perfect truth, 'I'm not looking forward to having to tell Richard how things are. It's sure to come as an awful shock.'

'He's certainly not going to like the fact that the woman he thought of as his is really mine,' Quinn commented, with what sounded remarkably like triumph. 'However, I might let him have the diamond as a consolation prize...'

Catching Elizabeth's expression, Quinn paused. 'But perhaps you don't want him to have it? Maybe you'd prefer to keep it?'

'No, I certainly wouldn't.'

'Then why the frown?'

'I thought that was a very callous thing to say,' she muttered. 'Poor Richard's bound to be hurt and miserable...'

'It's my opinion that he would have been a damn sight more hurt and miserable if you *had* gone ahead and married him...

'At first I was jealous as hell every time his name was mentioned. Then I realized, despite your efforts to convince us both to the contrary, that any feelings you had for him were lukewarm, rather than passionate... And I strongly believe that every man should have a wife who genuinely loves him.'

'With the exception of yourself?' The words were out before she could stop them.

115

Apparently unruffled, Quinn observed, 'You may not love me, but at a guess I should say you feel a lot more for me than you do for him.'

She was unable to deny the charge.

For Richard she had felt a straightforward liking and respect and a growing fondness. The feelings she had for Quinn went a great deal deeper, were far more complex and ambivalent... A combination of love and something close to hate; a yearning to be with him, vying with the need to escape; a wealth of warmth and tenderness, coupled with a passionate resentment that he thought so ill of her.

Quinn watched her through his lashes, as though expecting a contradiction, but, biting her lip, she stayed silent.

'I presume you'll want to talk to Beaumont before we start for the States?' he asked after a moment.

'Yes.' She must talk to Richard as soon as possible, but she had no intention of going to the States, or anywhere else, with Quinn. Though a sense of self-preservation warned that this was no time to say so.

It would be a great deal more prudent to pretend to go along with his plans until she was safely back in Cantle Cottage with the door locked against him...

'Confessing to your fiancé that you already have a husband isn't something you can really do over the phone,' Quinn went on, 'so that means waiting until he gets back from Amsterdam.

'Even so,' he added with satisfaction, 'we should be able to travel, say, Wednesday or Thursday at the latest. If we fly Concorde to New York I might even be able to take my seat at the World Banking Conference before we begin our honeymoon proper.

'And, speaking of honeymoons, I wondered about Hawaii as a possible destination? Unless you can think of anywhere else you'd specially like to go?'

Seeing he was waiting for an answer, she murmured that

Hawaii sounded wonderful, and, afraid he'd read her face, rose and began to clear the table.

She was putting the dishes in the sink when, pushing back his chair, he queried, 'Need any help?'

'No, thank you,' she answered politely, and, taking care not to look in his direction, heard him leave the kitchen.

Through the window she could see grey mist hanging over the now neglected garden, and a bank of thicker fog lying out at sea. If they didn't leave soon the journey back to London could well be a hazardous one.

As soon as everything was in order, Elizabeth dried her hands and hurried up to her room for her case and shoulder-bag. Leaving them in the hall, she went in search of him.

She was both surprised and dismayed to find all the lights were on in the study and a cheerful fire was burning.

Showing every sign of being settled for the day, Quinn was sitting at the desk glancing through a miscellaneous pile of notebooks.

When he looked up, she asked with more impatience than she'd intended to show, 'Shouldn't we be leaving soon?'

'What's the rush?' he asked mildly.

'Well, we...we don't want to miss the tide... And the fog shows every sign of getting worse.'

'It's no great tragedy if we're forced to stay. Though our meals may be a little bohemian, we're not likely to starve.'

'No, but I...I'd like to get back.'

'Any particular reason for the hurry?'

'I don't feel comfortable here,' she said in a rush. 'If you remember, I didn't want to come in the first place.'

'Guilty conscience?' he asked succinctly.

'No,' she denied.

His face a little stern above the black polo shirt, he suggested, 'In that case why don't you sit down in front of the fire until I've had a look through this lot?'

As, seeing nothing else for it, she took a seat, he queried, 'By the way, do you know if Henry kept a diary?'

She shook her head. 'I don't think so. I know he did a lot of writing, but I never saw him with anything resembling a diary.'

Quinn returned his attention to the task in hand, while Elizabeth did her best to possess her soul in patience.

After a little while the inactivity began to fray her nerves. Glancing up, she saw Quinn's eyes were fixed on her thoughtfully. 'You seem restless.'

'I feel restless,' she admitted.

'You used to be a great reader, and there are plenty of books.'

'I couldn't settle to reading.' With a great deal of truth, she admitted, 'I keep thinking of all the things I have to do when we get back to town.'

'Such as?'

Needing convincing reasons for returning as soon as possible, she said, 'I must let Lady Beaumont know I won't be going back... Then there's the cottage to clean through, and I'll have to make arrangements about the keys and find someone else to keep an eye on the place... And of course there are things like credit card statements and bills to be paid...

'The more I think about it, the more there seems to be to get done. In fact I'm beginning to doubt if I can be ready in time...'

Still watching her, Quinn said nothing.

Flustered by that narrow-eyed, assessing look, she stumbled on, 'But as you have a seat at the World Banking Conference you could always go on ahead...'

'I think not.' There was a little edge to his voice, a certain grimness that suggested he didn't altogether trust her apparent capitulation.

As if to prove it, he added wryly, 'The last time I went

back to the States and left you alone I returned to find the bird had flown…'

'Oh, but I—'

'Then, I had very little choice. I couldn't let my uncle lose the bank he'd been head of for the whole of his working life.

'This time, however, I have no such debt of gratitude to repay, and I have every intention of putting personal considerations before business.'

Trenchantly, he added, 'Experience has taught me a valuable lesson, and I never make the same mistake twice…'

It was a pity she couldn't boast the same, Elizabeth thought vexedly. If she hadn't been weak enough to give in to him a second time, she wouldn't be caught in this trap.

'No, my sweet Jo, I intend to be by your side day and night until I'm satisfied that you really do mean to stay with me.'

'How cosy.'

'Do I detect a sour note?'

'It makes you seem like a gaoler.'

Shrugging, he answered, 'Needs must,' and returned to his perusal of the notebooks.

With a sinking heart she faced the fact that simply going back to Cantle Cottage and locking him out—if she could—wasn't going to work. As long as he knew where she was, he wouldn't give up, and if he laid siege to the place, what then?

He couldn't *force* her to go back with him, but she would be fighting herself as well as him, and how long could she hold out?

Somehow she must get away from him, and the sooner the better. Every moment they were together found her deeper in his toils. Soon she wouldn't have the strength to go, and she couldn't bear to live with a man who despised her.

It seemed the only way to be free of him was to disappear as swiftly and completely as she had done before.

Though for most of the time she had lived without happiness or pleasure or laughter, but with an almost constant ache of regret for what might have been, she had survived.

And she could do it again. *If* she could get away.

But the last time she had taken him by surprise. This time it would be so much harder. From what he'd just said, even when they were back in London, he had no intention of leaving her side…

As she mulled over the possibilities, a daring thought struck her. Could she possibly slip away now, while he was occupied? If she could take the car, even though it was foggy, she ought to be back in town by early evening.

He would almost certainly follow her by whatever means he could… But with a head start it should be possible to pick up her few belongings, leave the Mercedes outside the cottage, and disappear before he arrived on the scene.

Yes, it might just work. It was certainly her best chance. *So long as she could find the car keys and take care not to miss the tide…*

Roused into action, she jumped to her feet.

Looking up, Quinn enquired idly, 'Going somewhere?'

Her brain suddenly icily clear, her answer came pat. 'Yesterday you mentioned that you wanted to clear the house… I thought while I needed something to occupy me I'd go and sort through the clothes and things that are still in my room. I'll put them in bags for some charity or other…'

Her voice as casual as she could make it, she asked, 'Have you any idea how long you'll be?'

'I doubt if I'll be finished in time to get across today. I want to look at these, and I still have to go through the contents of the safe and find the brooch Henry wanted you to have.'

Cocking an eyebrow, he added, 'I hope you don't mind *too* much if we have to spend another night here?'

It might be exactly what she needed. If she could get safely over and leave him stranded here it would give her even more time.

'No, I don't mind.' Realizing she'd sounded far too eager, she bit her lip and, trying to appear reluctant but resigned, added, 'It's no use minding if it can't be helped.'

Then, to allay any possible suspicions, she said, 'I'll have a look through the freezer and see what I can find for our evening meal. Is there anything in particular you fancy?'

'Not really. Surprise me.'

With a bit of luck she'd do just that.

The jacket she'd been wearing the previous day was lying over a chair. It was the only coat she had with her, but if she picked it up it might arouse his suspicions... She would manage without it.

As she turned towards the door, he said, 'Come and give me a kiss before you go.'

His hair a little rumpled, as though he'd been running his fingers through it, a stray lock falling over his forehead, he looked boyish and oddly vulnerable.

Elizabeth had a sudden vivid picture of his early years, the child he must have been. Young, sensitive, desperate to be loved and wanted after his mother's death, feeling abandoned by the next woman he'd given his love to, and rejected by his father...

It was a blessing his aunt and uncle had loved and wanted him. Even so, his earlier experience must have left some scars.

Walking over to the desk, she stooped to kiss his cheek. She felt an almost maternal tenderness, and a great sadness that he couldn't care for her as she cared for him.

'I was expecting a proper kiss,' he complained, as she straightened.

Her stomach clenching as though a lift had dropped, it occurred to her that this might be the last time she would ever kiss him.

She bent and kissed his lips. Firm, chiselled lips that could soften into sensuality, and spark off a wild hunger, but which at the moment were quiescent beneath hers.

'That's better,' he muttered. And, suddenly all man, with a movement she was unprepared for he pulled her on to his knee and deepened the kiss, sending both her senses and her sense of purpose reeling.

With a tremendous effort of will she pulled away, her grey eyes clouded with emotion. The lure was sweet...but, if she took it, before long only bitterness would be left.

When he would have kissed her again, she put her fingers over his mouth. 'We've both got work to do,' she said huskily. 'If we go on like this we'll *never* get back to London.'

'I didn't realize what an eminently sensible woman I'd married.' Sighing, he let her go.

Trying to look casual, unhurried, she made her way to the door, and though she knew his eyes were on her she refused to look back.

As soon as the door was safely closed behind her, she went up to his room as quickly as possible. The olive-green jacket and sweater he'd been wearing when they arrived were hanging over the back of a chair.

Trying not to feel like the thief he thought her, she searched hastily through the jacket pockets. They yielded a wallet, an international driving licence, a small comb, a pocket knife and a folded handkerchief. Then, just as she was giving up hope, a set of keys.

The sudden blaze of excitement fizzled out as she realized they were house keys. So where had he put the car keys?

Without much hope she went through his grip. It contained nothing but his evening wear and a couple of changes of clothing. A quick look round the room also proved fruitless.

The car keys were almost certainly in his trouser pocket. That left only one thing to do: she must walk across.

Then what?

A train? Or perhaps someone would have a car she could hire? Though both those options would almost certainly take time... And, as soon as he realized she was gone, if the causeway was still clear, he'd follow her.

Well, she'd just have to pray that he missed the tide. She didn't dare think about the alternative... Unless... Jenny Hicks!

While she'd been living at Saltmarsh, Jenny had been the town's librarian, and they'd become good friends. Jenny's parents had kept a small, but cheerful, bed and breakfast place quite close to the shore.

Of course that was over five years ago, but the family were local, born and bred in Saltmarsh, which made it unlikely that they would have moved.

To the best of her knowledge, Quinn knew nothing about them, so she'd be safe hiding out there until she was sure he'd gone. Then she could make her way to London, or some other big town, where it would be easy to disappear. She had money and credit cards with her...

Thoughts racing, she crept downstairs and picked up her shoulder-bag. It seemed best to leave her case. She would get on faster without it, and if Quinn should come through the hall its presence might help to lull any suspicions.

Jenny would probably be happy to lend her anything she needed until she'd had a chance to do some shopping...

The hinges of the heavy front door groaned a little as

she opened it, making her hold her breath. When there was no sign of movement from the study, she gave a sigh of relief and pulled the door to quietly behind her.

As soon as she was outside, the raw, foggy air wrapped around her, making her shiver. But if she walked fast enough, she told herself bracingly, she wouldn't feel the cold.

The car was still standing in front of the garages, where Quinn had left it, and, with a sigh of regret, she hurried past it and down the paved incline, glad that the study was on the other side of the house.

But even if Quinn had been able to look out in that direction he would have had a job to see her. It was a lot foggier than she'd realized. Reaching the shoreline, she glanced back. The house was only a dark, featureless bulk in the murk.

From somewhere close at hand an invisible sea bird called mournfully. It was answered by the harsh, mewing cry of a gull.

Teeth chattering, and already chilled to the bone, she looked ahead. Some half-mile away, on the mainland, partly obscured by the grey, shifting curtain, the lights of the town signalled warmth and shelter.

Thanking heaven that she was wearing flat-heeled shoes, and taking care to watch the thin white poles that, planted at intervals, marked the edges of the causeway, she made what speed she could, alternately walking and running, her thoughts keeping pace.

Having to do it this way meant she dared not go back to Cantle Cottage, because Quinn was sure to have it watched. But she had nothing there she couldn't bear to leave behind. At least for the time being...

A stitch in her side made her pause for a moment to catch her breath, before hurrying on.

At the first opportunity she would have to call Australia

and ask Emily Henderson what she wanted to do about the keys, and finding a new caretaker for the cottage...

A worse problem was breaking the news to Richard. Though uncertain just how much she would need to tell him, she would have to write as soon as possible and let him know the engagement was off.

It seemed a cowardly way to do it, but she wouldn't dare try to see him. Quinn would be waiting for just that very thing...

The causeway, which on a fine summer day was no distance at all, now seemed an awful long way, and though she kept moving as fast as possible she felt almost paralyzed with cold.

And surely the visibility was getting much worse? With a sudden shock of fear she realized that within the last few seconds the white poles stretching ahead had disappeared. So had the lights of the town.

A bank of denser fog rolling in from the sea had overtaken her silently, stealthily, a smothering blanket, deadening sound and obscuring everything.

Fighting down raw-edged panic, she tried to think logically. The only thing she could do was keep going. She couldn't be too far from the mainland. Once she was off the causeway and away from the sea, visibility was almost certain to improve.

Taking short steps, her hands spread in front of her as though she were blind, she began to move cautiously forward, doing her best to keep in a straight line.

She had been going for perhaps a minute when it dawned on her that the ground beneath her feet was the slightly yielding texture of damp sand, rather than the concrete of the causeway.

As she stopped abruptly and hesitated, she found her shoes were wet. She was just digesting this frightening fact when a sudden surge of icy water swirled around her ankles and sucked sand from beneath her feet.

Flailing to keep her balance, she felt the strap of her bag slip from her shoulder. Unable to see a thing, she stooped and was groping about, trying to find it, when another wave engulfed her arms up to her elbows, and threatened to take her feet from under her.

Giving up the search, she straightened and turned to retrace her steps, only to find that she was splashing in even deeper water.

Completely disoriented, she stood quite still. But there wasn't much time, common sense warned. The tide swept in quickly on this flat stretch of coast.

Galvanized by that chilling thought, she had taken a few desperate steps when an even more horrifying thought brought her to a halt and made her heart start to pound with slow, heavy thuds.

When she had first come to Saltmarsh she had been warned never to stray from the causeway because of dangerous quicksands. There was a local legend to the effect that in Victorian times they had swallowed up an unwary rider and his horse.

Oh, dear God, what was she to do?

'Jo!' The muffled shout seemed to echo and ricochet off the walls of fog.

She tried to answer, but only managed a croak.

'Jo!' This time Quinn's shout was closer, and she saw through the grey mass the brightness of a hand-held flare.

'I'm here! Off the causeway.' She was unable to keep the panic from her voice.

'Don't move. Stay exactly where you are and start counting. One, two...'

With the fog masking sight and deadening sound it was impossible to tell just how close he was, and already the water was eddying round her calves, making her flounder repeatedly.

But she trusted Quinn implicitly. Her eyes fixed on the moving pinkish-orange glow, she took up the count. 'Three, four…'

She had reached fifteen when the flare went out. 'Quinn!'

Her involuntary cry of alarm was answered by a reassuring, 'It's all right. I'm here.' A second or two later a dark shape loomed out of the fog, and he was by her side.

'Give me your hand.' He began to lead her with a certainty she could only marvel at, and after a few floundering steps she felt the concrete of the causeway beneath her feet.

'Take hold of my arm and turn your head away.'

Keeping a tight grip on his arm, she did as she'd been bidden, and out of the corner of her eye saw another flare burst into brilliant life.

The pinkish glow illuminated the curtain of fog, briefly picking out one of the marker posts and gleaming on the dark ripples.

One hand holding it aloft, the other securely round her waist, he said, 'The tide's coming in fast; we'll have to hurry.'

Though his voice was calm, she recognized the underlying urgency. Her whole body icy cold, her feet dead, she did her best, but the swirling water was knee-deep now, and getting deeper.

She stumbled, and, muttering something under his breath, Quinn urged her forward. Knowing his life was at stake as well as her own, she gritted her teeth and battled on.

But in her numb and weakened state it was like wading through treacle, and her reserves of strength were fast running out. He was half carrying her, when all at once it began to get easier.

With a fresh heart she forced her reluctant legs to keep

moving, and in a few yards they were at the end of the causeway and splashing through the shallows.

As soon as they were safe on the gritty sand above high water mark, her knees buckled under her and she sat down abruptly.

Setting the flare down on the sand, Quinn stripped off his jacket and sweater. Then, hauling Elizabeth to her feet, he pulled the sweater over her head and zipped her into the jacket.

They still held the warmth of his body and almost immediately some of the dreadful paralysis began to leave her.

'Let's get going before hypothermia sets in,' he said briskly. As he spoke the flare spluttered and died.

'Have you another one?' She was surprised how normal her voice sounded.

'No, but we can manage from here. We'll soon be on the road.' He put an arm round her and led her into the murk.

Hardly able to see a hand in front of her, she wondered whether it was instinct, or pure confidence, that allowed him to move with such relative ease.

When the foreshore had been left behind them and the subsequent hard-packed, rutted ground had given way to tarmac, Quinn breathed a sigh of relief. 'Not far now. We should be able to see the lights of the inn before too long.'

In a couple of minutes he was proved right, and a short time later he was opening the door of the Ship and pushing her into the lounge where a cheerful fire was blazing.

The man who had served them the previous day was polishing glasses at the bar. He looked surprised. 'Didn't expect any customers on an afternoon like this.'

Then, taking in Quinn's shirt-sleeves and wet trousers, their soaking footwear and Elizabeth's white-faced, exhausted state, he exclaimed, 'You've obviously been in trouble! What do you need?'

'Hot coffee first and foremost.'

The landlord disappeared without another word.

After leading Elizabeth to a chair close by the fire, Quinn stooped to pull off her sodden shoes and chafe her icy feet between his palms.

Her wet things were steaming gently in the heat when a rattle of cups announced the arrival of the coffee.

A buxom woman with soft brown hair and a fresh complexion put the tray on the nearest table. 'I've made a whole pot. My husband said you'd had trouble?'

Quinn rose to his feet to pour the coffee and put a cup into Elizabeth's hand, before answering matter-of-factly, 'My wife and I had started to cross the causeway when the fog thickened and slowed us down, and we were almost caught by the tide.'

The landlady tutted sympathetically. 'It comes in very fast in these parts. It's a miracle no one's been drowned. I take it you're from the big house?'

'Yes.'

Getting down to practicalities, she observed, 'Well, you'll not get back today, so you'll be wanting a hot bath and a room for the night?'

'Please.'

'Number three has its own bathroom. I'll pop up and light a fire—there's central heating, of course, but a fire's a lot more cheerful—and make sure you have everything there you need.'

Glancing at Elizabeth's chalk-white face, she remarked kindly, 'You look absolutely done in. If you'd like any help...'

'Thank you, but I'll be fine.'

Turning back to Quinn, she suggested, 'You'll be wanting a full evening meal rather than a bar snack? Steak and kidney pudding and apple pie to follow?'

'Sounds marvellous.'

'I'll bring up a tray about seven.' She added, 'If you'd like me to wash and dry your wet things, just let me have them.' She took herself off.

The coffee was hot and strong and more than welcome. By the time Elizabeth had gulped down two cups, the terrible inner coldness had gone and life was starting to come back to her frozen limbs.

'More coffee?' Quinn asked.

She shook her head.

'Then I suggest you get out of those wet clothes and into a hot bath.'

On struggling to her feet, she found her legs were so shaky they would barely support her, and the pain of returning circulation was making her eyes fill with water.

Quinn, who missed nothing, was by her side in an instant.

'I'm sorry,' she whispered. 'I've got hot-aches. I'm not crying.' As if to give the lie to that statement, twin tears overflowed and rolled slowly down her cheeks.

Quinn muttered something under his breath and, scooping her up in his arms, set off for the stairs.

She could feel the tension in every muscle of his body, and a quick, nervous glance at his face told her that he was absolutely *livid*.

Suddenly, scared to be alone with him, she wished she'd accepted the landlady's offer of help.

But it would only have been a postponement. She would have had to face his anger sooner or later.

CHAPTER EIGHT

BY THE time they reached their room, where a fire had already been lit and a basket of logs placed by the hearth, she was trembling in every limb.

'I don't know what's the matter with me.' She was aware she sounded apologetic.

'Delayed shock.' He gave his opinion curtly. Carrying her into the bathroom, he set her down carefully on a stool, and turned on the taps.

The landlady had been as good as her word. Next to a fresh pile of towels were two white towelling robes and two complimentary packs of toilet articles, which contained everything they might need.

When the bath was full, and fragrant steam rising, Quinn stripped off Elizabeth's clothes and helped her step in. All the stuffing gone out of her, and still shaking, she submitted to his ministrations like an exhausted child.

When her head was settled against the headrest, and she was enveloped in the comforting warmth, he asked, 'Okay?'

'Fine, thank you.'

'Is there anything else you'd like me to do?'

Concerned for him now, she said, 'Yes, I'd like you to get out of your own wet things.'

'Will you be all right if I take a shower?'

'Quite all right, thank you.'

His anger was under control now and hidden, and they were talking to each other with a kind of stilted politeness.

'Don't go to sleep,' he warned.

'I won't,' she promised.

131

Through half-closed eyes, she watched him strip off his black polo shirt and saturated trousers, admiring his splendid physique and the smooth ripple of muscles.

She could only thank heaven that he was the kind of man he was, that his will-power and courage matched his physical strength.

In those conditions, a lesser man might never have come looking for her, let alone risked his own life to save her...

Before long she started to feel relaxed and drowsy and the shaking stopped. By the time Quinn had showered and put on the towelling robe, in spite of her promise, she was half asleep.

Dabbling a hand in the rapidly cooling water, he pulled out the plug and said briskly, 'Time you were out of there and into bed.'

Helping her to her feet, he wrapped a large, fluffy bath towel round her and effortlessly lifted her out. 'Do you want any help, or can you manage now?'

Somewhat dazed, but on her dignity, she said, 'I can manage, thank you.'

'Then I'll take these down.' He gathered up their wet things and went out, leaving the door slightly ajar.

Watching his retreating back, she found she was disappointed. Without in the least understanding her own feelings, her sudden sense of dependency—if that was what it was—she had hoped he would dry her.

Her arms curiously leaden, she dried herself, rubbing the bedraggled ends of her hair and combing it, before pulling on the waiting robe.

When she went through to the bedroom—the same room she and Quinn had shared previously—it was warm and cosy, the bedside lamps were lit and the fire in the black grate was blazing cheerfully.

Quinn wasn't back, and all at once she felt alone and lonely. Which was stupid, she thought, climbing into bed.

She was good at being alone. Anyone could get good at being alone with enough practice. And she'd had quite a lot of practice...

But what a sad way to spend one's life.

No matter what Quinn might believe, she had never cared about material things. The only thing she'd ever really wanted out of life was just to love and be loved in return.

The one thing it seemed she could never have...

All at once tears welled up in her eyes. Too weary to hold them back, she let them spill over and run down her cheeks in tracks of shiny wetness.

The bed was comfortable, the pillows soft, and when Quinn returned a minute or so later she was fast asleep, her black hair spread across the pillow, her pale face still wet with tears.

He stood looking down at her, his expression bleak, before moving to sit by the fire.

A knock at the door wakened Elizabeth, and she sat up dazedly to find the fire had been replenished and their dinner had arrived.

When the tray of food had been set on a low table by the hearth, the landlady said, 'I'll be up in half an hour or so to clear away and bring the coffee. If you need anything else in the meantime, just let me know.'

Quinn thanked her, and she bustled away.

Turning to Elizabeth, he said with distant civility, 'You still look exhausted. Would you like your meal in bed?'

Feeling groggy, her stomach balking at the thought of food, she would have liked to just go quietly back to sleep again. But, unwilling to admit her weakness, she said with forced brightness, 'I'm as right as rain, thank you. I'd much sooner get up.'

'If that's what you prefer.'

Once again they were talking to each other like polite but wary strangers.

Climbing out of bed, she tightened the belt of her robe and came to sit by the fire.

The home-cooked food was excellent, but she could only manage a few mouthfuls. Quinn too ate sparingly, his face cold and aloof, his musings clearly sombre ones.

Wishing she could see beneath that icy façade, she wondered just what he was thinking, feeling, planning.

By the time the landlady had brought the coffee and departed with the dirty dishes, more than an hour had passed, and except for thanking that good lady he hadn't spoken a single word.

A barbed-wire tension filled the air, stretching between them, putting Elizabeth on tenterhooks.

Leaning forward, he picked up the coffee pot, and, having filled two cups with the fragrant brew, proceeded to drain his own in silence.

Her nerves at breaking point, and unable to bear the strain a moment longer, she burst out hoarsely, 'I haven't thanked you yet for…'

He looked up, and, shaken rigid by the expression in his green eyes, she faltered to a halt. When he said nothing, desperate to make some kind of contact, she admitted, 'I— I know you're angry with me but—'

With a sudden savage fury that was more daunting because it was quiet, he snarled, 'Angry doesn't begin to cover it. What you did was absolutely idiotic! If I hadn't realized you'd gone, you could have died out there.'

'Not could have. Would have.' Her voice was unsteady, close to tears. 'You saved my life.'

A white line appearing around his mouth, he said, 'You must absolutely loathe me to have risked it.'

'No!'

He laughed harshly. 'There's little point in denying it.

It's clear you find the thought of being married to me quite insupportable.

'I was an arrogant fool to think for a moment that sharing my bed meant you were willing to stay with me. If I hadn't been so damned cock-a-hoop I'd have realized from your manner that you had no intention of going through with it.

'Perhaps, underneath, I never really believed your apparent surrender. Maybe that was what made me uneasy enough to go up to your room...

'When you weren't there, I looked in the kitchen... Then I saw that though your case was still in the hall your handbag was missing... You did take it?'

'Yes.'

'What happened to it?'

'I lost it. The strap slipped off my shoulder. I couldn't see, so I tried feeling for it, but the water was getting deeper and I panicked.'

His face grim, he said, 'No wonder.'

'I knew I had to keep moving, but I didn't know which way to go. If you hadn't caught up with me soon after that...' Shuddering violently, she let the words tail off.

'It was a miracle I did. When I saw the car was where I'd left it, I thought you must still be in the house somewhere. I could hardly believe that anyone in their right mind would be reckless enough to start out on foot on a day like this, and with the tide already on the turn. If it hadn't been for that missing bag...'

He passed a hand over his eyes. Then, roughly, he asked, 'Tell me, if you were so determined to go, why walk? You can drive, can't you?'

'Yes, I can drive. A college friend who had an old banger taught me.'

'Then why didn't you take the car?'

'I couldn't find the keys,' she admitted. 'I presumed you must have them on you.'

'Would you believe I'd left them in the ignition?'

Ironically, it was the one place she'd never thought to look. It seemed fate had been laughing at her.

Wanting to keep him talking so he could rid himself of some of the bitterness and anger that was riding him, she asked, 'Why didn't *you* use the car?'

'By then it was too foggy to chance driving across. For one thing I might have knocked you down. In any case, as soon as I remembered there used to be flares in the boat-house, I knew if I could find them I'd make better time on foot.'

'Thank God you did,' she said with fervour. 'When I realized I'd strayed off the causeway, I've never been so scared in my life. Especially when I remembered the quick-sand...'

His face a mask, the olive skin stretched tightly over the strong bones, he said, 'I take it you intended to head for London?'

'Yes.'

'Had you decided to throw yourself on Beaumont's tender mercies.'

'No.'

'So you'd planned to disappear again?'

Biting her lip, she admitted, 'Yes. But not because I hated you. I've never hated you. I left you the first time because I couldn't bear to stay with a man who thought so ill of me.

'If I'd been the sort of woman you imagined, it wouldn't have *mattered* what you thought of me, so long as you could provide the desired lifestyle. But it *did* matter.'

His eyes had become guarded, his expression shuttered, and it was impossible to judge whether or not she'd succeeded in getting through to him

After a moment, he asked, 'And this time?'

'Nothing had changed. You continued to regard me as a

heartless gold-digger.' Half hoping for a rebuttal, she added, 'No doubt you still do.'

But, nothing if not honest, he merely asked, 'So where does that leave us?'

'I don't know,' she answered.

He stared into the fire for what seemed an age, before saying slowly, 'It isn't easy to rid oneself of preconceived notions, and everything pointed to it being the truth.

'All the same I was starting to have second thoughts about some aspects of your relationship with Henry. Unless you're a consummate liar, things weren't adding up...'

She felt a little flicker of hope.

'But until I can find some *proof* of how you two felt about each other there'll always be room for doubt...'

The little flicker of hope died.

'And would he have left half his fortune to just any pretty girl who'd been his secretary for so short a time? I doubt it. He wasn't a fool. Unless you subscribe to the "there's no fool like an old fool" school of thought. So he must have had some *reason*...

'You say your relationship was platonic; that you went to his room to play chess; that he wasn't angry when you told him you were running off to marry me—'

'And all of that's true.' She fought back. 'Don't forget it was *after* I'd gone that he made his will.'

'Perhaps he was hoping to lure you back. If he *was* besotted with you, he might have thought that if you were through with me he could have you for himself...'

'That's obscene,' she burst out. 'I was married to his *son*.'

'Perhaps he didn't see that as an insurmountable obstacle. Maybe he knew the marriage hadn't been consummated and could be annulled...

'But if I hadn't been forced to fly back to the States at a moment's notice it no doubt *would* have been consummated. So how could he have known it hadn't been? Unless you were lying all along…'

As she opened her mouth to protest, he went on, 'Suppose you *hadn't* told him we were getting married…suppose, when it was too late, he got wind of it some other way, and, in a last desperate bid to get you back, came up to London, and out of jealousy gave you his version of why I'd married you?'

'He didn't.'

'Tell me the truth, Jo.'

'That *is* the truth.'

'Though I was unable to get any details, I know *someone* called at the flat that night after I'd gone.'

'It wasn't Henry.'

'Then who was it? If you want me to believe you it's time you started answering some questions.'

Perhaps her defences were down for, without really intending to, she found herself admitting, 'It was Piery.'

'Piery!'

Just for an instant Quinn looked like a man who had received a knockout blow. Then a mask was firmly in place, hiding thoughts and emotions alike.

After a moment or two, his voice cool and controlled, he said, 'So it was Piery who called on you that night. I ought to have realized earlier. It's the one explanation that makes sense… Why did you refuse to tell me before?'

'I—I didn't want you to know. I was afraid it would cause even more discord in the family.'

There was a pause while he seemed to weigh up and evaluate her reasoning. Then, carefully, he said, 'There's something I find strange. If you were as innocent of blame as you're trying to make out, why were you so ready to believe everything Piery told you? It doesn't—'

'I didn't want to believe *any* of it,' she broke in desperately, 'but I *had* to. He showed me a letter you'd written to him after your first visit to Saltmarsh. There was no doubt it was your writing…'

When Quinn would have interrupted, she rushed on, 'Let me tell you what it said…'

Even after more than five years those damning words were branded on her brain in letters of fire.

'It said, "Don't worry, I'll be back again in a week or so. Now I've seen for myself just what she's up to, and how besotted Henry is, I'll put a stop to her little games, even if it means marrying her myself. Someone should teach her a lesson…" Do you deny writing that?'

'No, I don't deny it,' he said flatly. 'That was how I felt at the time.'

With magnificent understatement, she admitted, 'It came as something of a shock.' She had felt pierced to the heart, as if every last drop of blood was draining from her body. 'I didn't know what to do.'

'It didn't take you long to decide. I understand you left the flat shortly afterwards.'

'Piery helped me. He took me to the nearest hotel and booked me a room.'

'And you saw the family lawyers next morning?'

'Yes. Piery suggested that the marriage should be annulled and gave me their address.'

'He seems to have been invaluable.'

Stiffly, she said, 'Piery was very good. He even offered to stay with me until I'd got myself together, and was able to think straight.'

'And did he?'

'I refused to let him. For one thing I needed to be alone.'

'Go on,' Quinn said grimly. 'And don't leave anything out.'

Too weary to dissemble, she spoke the exact truth. 'He asked how long you'd be away, and when I told him a couple of days he suggested that to save a lot of hassle I

should disappear before you got back. He said he would
help me find a bedsit and a job of some kind—'

A white line appeared around Quinn's mouth. 'Are you
saying he *knew* where you were?'

She shook her head. 'No. I didn't want to involve him.
I thought it better to make a clean break. Though I felt bad
about disappearing without a word when he'd gone to so
much trouble—'

His face grim, Quinn asked, 'Did he ever tell you *why*
he'd gone to so much trouble?'

'He said he felt to blame, and he was angry that he hadn't
shown me the letter earlier, before we were married. But
he knew nothing about the wedding until it was too late.
He came up to London as soon as he found out.'

Frowning, Quinn observed, 'There's one thing that puzzles me. How did Piery know I'd gone to the States and
you'd be on your own?'

She had started to droop visibly, and it took an effort of
will to lift her head and answer, 'He overheard a telephone
conversation between your uncle and Henry...

'When William discovered how his business rivals were
planning to stab him in the back he tried to get in touch
with you at Saltmarsh.

'Henry told him you were being married that very afternoon, and staying the night at your flat before going on
honeymoon.

'Finding it was your wedding day, William balked at
disturbing you. But when Henry realized your casting vote
was urgently needed to save the bank he said he was sure
that as soon as you knew how things stood you'd move
heaven and earth to get on a flight immediately...'

And it had been a close thing. As soon as William had
phoned and briefly explained the situation, Quinn had rung
the airport and managed to get a single seat on a plane
leaving in less than an hour.

'It's a toss-up whether I'll get there in time,' he'd told her, 'but I have to try. You do understand?'

Well aware that it was a matter of loyalty, she'd said immediately, 'Of course I understand.'

'If you don't hear from me, you'll know I'm on the flight.' He'd kissed her hard. 'I'll be back tomorrow or the day after.'

He had been gone less than two hours when Piery had arrived, and all her happiness and hopes for the future had been so brutally torn apart...

'You look absolutely weary.' Quinn's voice broke into her thoughts. 'It's time you were in bed for the night.'

Giving up all pretence, she was only too pleased to clean her teeth and crawl beneath the duvet.

Quinn turned out the lamps, leaving only the firelight, and took her place in the bathroom. She heard the taps running, but when he emerged instead of getting into bed, he went back to sit by the fire.

The room was comfortably dim and cosy. But, tired as she was, her brain stubbornly refused to switch off, and she found herself unable to sleep.

When the grandfather clock on the landing whirred self-importantly and struck ten, she was still wide awake, lying staring up at the painted mermaids on the ceiling. Waiting.

Remembering how last time she'd watched them from the haven of Quinn's arms, she felt an aching sadness.

Though he was only yards away, she knew he was deliberately shutting her out, and once more she felt terribly alone.

Earlier, he'd asked, 'Where does that leave us?' And she'd been unable to answer him. So where *did* it leave them? Now *she* needed an answer.

Nothing had changed... Even as she reminded herself, she knew that that was no longer true. The situation might not have changed, but *she* had.

For the sake of her pride she had run away from Quinn not once but twice...

But pride was a cold bedfellow. And what was pride compared to happiness, however brief?

Being with him—as things were—was unlikely to mean complete, unsullied happiness. Any happiness they found together might not only be short-lived, but might well end in sadness.

Yet it had to be better than the living death of being without him...

Life was a precious gift. Only now, when she'd so nearly lost it, did she realize just *how* precious. A gift to be enjoyed, and shared, and, if possible, lived to the full.

She turned her head to look at him. In the dying glow of the fire, his face looked cold and unapproachable, the jaw firm, the chiselled mouth set.

But when he was lying next to her, and she told him of her change of heart, surely those icy barriers would melt?

She sighed. If only he'd come to bed...

As though she had spoken the thought aloud, he rose to his feet and, tossing aside the robe, got in beside her, careful not to touch her.

Wondering what to say, how best to broach the subject, she waited, hoping against hope that he would make the first move, or at least give her an opening of some kind.

But though he must have known she was wide awake he never even glanced in her direction. His breathing light and even, he lay staring up at the ceiling, much as she herself had been doing.

She was still hesitating when he turned on his side, his back to her.

Too late she found her voice. 'Quinn...?'

When he gave no sign of hearing her, remembering the old adage that actions speak louder than words, she plucked up courage and snuggled against his broad back, one smooth leg rubbing against the roughness of his.

She felt his whole body tense, but he neither moved nor spoke.

Determined to get some response, she put an arm around his waist and let her hand stroke down over his flat stomach.

With a sudden movement she was unprepared for he seized her hand and, thrusting it away, turned on her savagely. 'Damn you, are you trying to provoke me?'

Shrinking away from his anger, she said, 'I'm trying to get you to talk to me.'

Propped on one elbow, he threatened, 'If you're not very careful, the last thing I'll want to do is talk.'

Well, at least he still wanted her. Cheered by that knowledge, she said boldly, 'Well, I'll be happy to settle for a spot of non-verbal communication.'

'A final fling before you leave me again?'

Suddenly needing reassurance, she braced herself and asked, 'After all that's happened, do you want me to stay?'

'Yes, I want you to stay. God help me.'

'Then I will.'

'When did you make up your mind?' He sounded unconvinced. 'Earlier when I asked, Where does that leave us you said you didn't know.'

'Well, I—'

'You also said nothing had changed. Tell me, Jo, how long will it be before you decide to run again? Just as soon as you're able? As soon as you have the wherewithal?'

He shook his head. 'Much as I want you I can't face the strain of living with a woman who's likely to take off the first chance she gets.'

'I won't be taking off, as you put it.'

'Why not?' he asked bluntly. 'After all, you were quite right. Nothing has changed.'

'*I've* changed. Being so close to death made me realize how precious life is. It also made me realize that, no matter how difficult our relationship may be, I'd sooner live with you than without you.'

In the half-light she saw his face tighten in what seemed to be a spasm of pain. 'For how long?'

'This morning you suggested that we stayed together until the fever died.'

'And you're prepared to do that?'

'Yes.'

Though her answer was firm and decided, she knew he was far from convinced.

She lifted her face for his kiss, and after a brief, but telling, hesitation he kissed her lightly on the lips.

When she would have kissed him back, he said wryly, 'You really don't have to prove anything. Go to sleep. You look absolutely all in.'

Sighing inwardly, she faced the fact that though she'd gone some way to breaking down the barriers she hadn't achieved the closeness she'd sought. She had been hoping to sleep in his arms.

Feeling restless, dissatisfied, she moved back to her own side of the bed, and for what seemed an age lay without moving, listening to Quinn's quiet, even breathing, knowing that he too was wide awake.

She heard the clock strike one before she finally fell into an exhausted sleep.

The sound of a half-stifled scream brought her struggling and thrashing to the surface.

'It's all right, my love... Everything's all right. It was just a bad dream...'

Quinn's voice. Quinn's arms holding her securely. Sobbing for breath, her heart pounding, she lay against him, while he murmured soothingly, and the awful panic gradually subsided.

'I'm sorry,' she whispered. 'I hope I haven't disturbed anyone else.'

'Don't worry, I'm sure you haven't.'

'I was sinking in the quicksands...' She shuddered.

'Don't think about it.' Settling her head on his shoulder, he kissed her forehead. 'Go back to sleep. You're safe with me.'

'You won't let me go?'

'I won't let you go.'

Reassured, she closed her eyes, and this time her sleep was deep and peaceful.

Elizabeth stirred and woke to find herself alone in the big bed. She was absurdly disappointed.

Sitting up, she glanced round the bedroom. Both that and the bathroom, whose door stood ajar, were empty. There was no sign of Quinn.

Through the square panes of the bow-window she could see the fog had gone. A stiff breeze was moving the bare branches of some skeletal trees, and a watery sun was making a brave attempt to shine.

Despite the bright morning, the now familiar room had a somewhat forlorn look. White ashes filled the grate, and the remains of last night's coffee still stood on the hearth.

On a chest by the bed, in a neat pile, were her clothes and shoes. Her shoes had been dried and polished.

She was wondering what time it was when she heard the grandfather clock begin to strike. Like a child, she began to count...Ten, eleven, twelve... Twelve o'clock!

Where on earth was Quinn?

In all probability downstairs talking to the landlady. The voice of common sense overrode her sudden irrational alarm.

Getting out of bed, she pulled on the towelling robe, picked up her clothes, and headed for the bathroom.

Some ten minutes later, showered and dressed, a lack of hairpins forcing her to leave her hair loose around her shoulders, she was ready to go looking for him.

She was heading for the bedroom door when it opened and there he was, wearing his olive-green jacket, his dark hair a little rumpled by the wind. He was carrying her overnight case and a parcel wrapped in black plastic.

He came across to her and, hoping for a kiss, she smiled up at him.

'Good morning. How are you feeling?' His cool greeting was like a smack in the face.

Hiding her feeling of hurt as best she could, she said, 'As good as new... I—I don't know how I've managed to sleep so late.'

Putting her case on the chest, he remarked, 'Our landlady wanted to bring up some breakfast, but I thought it best not to disturb you.'

'You look as if you've been out and about.' Elizabeth's tone was falsely bright.

'As soon as the causeway was passable I walked over to fetch the car. On the way I kept an eye open and spotted this.'

Unwrapping the plastic, he produced her handbag. 'As you might expect, it's saturated and sandy. But with the compartments being zipped everything should be there. All it will need is careful drying out.'

'Thank you.' Taking it for him, she opened it, and breathed a glad sigh to find that both Henry's locket and the key to Cantle Cottage were safe. Her paper money was a soggy wodge, but her bank and credit cards, tucked snugly into the plastic compartments of a wallet, had fared remarkably well.

'Usable?' he queried.

'I think so.'

An odd note in his voice, he remarked, 'No doubt you'll be relieved to have them back.'

'Of course,' she agreed. 'But one of the things I'm most pleased to have back is the key to the cottage. It would have been awkward if I'd lost that. There is another one but it's—' Realizing that nervousness was making her babble, she broke off.

Glancing at his watch, he remarked, 'Lunch is waiting downstairs. You hardly ate a thing last night, so you must be ready for it?'

'Ready when you are.' She made an effort to sound cheerful.

'I've decided not to stay for lunch. I'd rather get on my way.'

A strange hollow feeling in the pit of her stomach, she stammered, 'B-but won't you be hungry?'

'I had a late breakfast.'

'Where are you going?'

'To London.'

'Without me?'

'There's some business I want to attend to. I thought you might prefer to stay here and rest.'

'When will you be back?' Then she said, with alarm, 'You *will* be back?'

'Yes. Tomorrow some time. I still have things to do at the house...

'By the way, the bill for this place has been taken care of, including tonight. And just in case you need any money before yours had dried out...' He placed a wad of notes beside her case.

So he hadn't believed she intended to stay with him, and he was offering her a chance to go.

No, more than a chance—he was almost encouraging her.

Why?

Was he just testing her? Or had he decided he no longer wanted her to stay with him?

The traumatic events of the previous day had altered *her* thinking. Had they also altered his?

But afterwards, when she'd asked him if he wanted her to stay, he'd said he did. And in the night, when she'd wakened with the nightmare, he'd called her 'my love'.

He hadn't *meant* it, of course, but just recalling the endearment warmed her and stiffened her resolve.

Picking up the money, she handed it back to him, and said crisply, 'Thank you, but I won't be needing this. I've every intention of coming to London with you.'

The veiled eyes studied her. 'Sure?'

'Quite sure,' she answered serenely.

'Would you like lunch before we go?'

She shook her head. 'I'll ask for some sandwiches to take with me.'

CHAPTER NINE

THE first part of the journey was accomplished in silence. Determined not to let it get on her nerves, Elizabeth ate the first of her sandwiches, and when Quinn refused a share demolished the second.

Having tidied away the crumbs and the cling film, she pulled the ring on a can of pop. It fizzed and foamed and ran down her fingers. The packet of tissues she usually carried in her handbag, reduced to a soggy mass by their immersion, had been thrown away.

'Can I borrow your hankie?' she asked.

'Presumably you know which pocket it's in,' he said wryly, 'so help yourself.'

Flushing a little, she felt in his nearest pocket and fished it out. Somehow the intimate little action made her—for the first time—feel like a wife.

Having wiped her sticky fingers, she offered him the can. 'Would you like some?'

He grimaced. 'I don't know how you can drink that stuff.'

'I'd sooner have had lager,' she admitted. 'But I didn't want to face Richard smelling of beer.'

'Were you thinking of seeing him this afternoon?'

'Yes— Though I'm dreading it,' she admitted.

'You don't have to go if you don't want to. I'm quite prepared to tell him how things stand.'

'No.' She couldn't be so cowardly. 'I have to tell him myself.'

'Then I'll go with you.'

'It might be better if I went alone.'

'If I'm any judge of character, Beaumont isn't a good loser—'

His assessment was more accurate than he knew, Elizabeth thought uneasily.

'In the circumstances no one could blame him for being angry, but I wouldn't like him to vent his anger on you.'

'Oh, but I—'

Quinn shook his head decidedly. 'You're my wife, and I intend to be there... Had you any particular time in mind for calling on him?'

'I'd prefer to get it over with as soon as possible.'

Taking her at her word, when they reached town, Quinn drove straight to Lombard Square. The square was quiet and pleasant, with elegant architecture and a central tree-lined garden, surrounded by black wrought-iron railings. Though it was only mid-afternoon, several of the big white houses had lighted chandeliers.

The imposing Georgian mansion which belonged to the Beaumonts stood on one corner. After parking in an area that stated 'Residents Only', Quinn helped Elizabeth out and escorted her to the door.

She went with mixed feelings. In one way, she would have preferred to see Richard alone. In another, she was only too pleased that Quinn had decided to put his foot down.

A smart, white-aproned maid answered their ring. At the sight of Elizabeth, the girl exclaimed, 'Why, Miss Cavendish, I'm afraid Lady Beaumont isn't home! I don't think she was...'

'Miss Cavendish is with me,' Quinn broke in coolly. 'My name's Durville.'

'Oh, yes, Mr Durville, you're expected. Please come this way.'

She led them across a handsomely furnished hall, tapped

on the study door, and ushered them inside. 'Miss Cavendish and Mr Durville.'

As the door closed behind the maid, Richard looked up from some papers he was studying. 'Durville.' He nodded coolly to Quinn. Then, rising from behind the leather-topped desk, he came over to kiss Elizabeth's cheek. 'Darling! This is a delightful surprise. I wasn't expecting to see you until tomorrow.

'I'm afraid Mother's out. I haven't broken the good news yet. I thought we could—'

On edge, she burst out, 'Richard, before you say anything, there's something I must tell you—'

Aware of his rival listening, he gave her a warning glance, and suggested, 'Can't it wait until we're alone?'

Running her tongue over dry lips, she said, 'It concerns Quinn.'

She saw Richard's almost imperceptible blink at the use of the other man's first name.

'Then perhaps you had better tell me.'

'Wh-when I said I didn't know him, it wasn't the truth. We first met over five years ago.'

Frowning, Richard demanded, 'Why lie about it?'

'I'm sorry, but seeing him again after all that time was a shock and I—'

'Do you mean you hadn't seen him for five years?'

'Yes.'

'Presumably, as seeing him affected you so strongly, your relationship had been somewhat more than platonic?'

'Yes.'

'That explains a great deal.' Then he asked sharply, 'Who ended it?'

'I did, but—'

Clearly relishing the idea of having the woman who had left his *bête noire*, Richard said magnanimously, 'My dear Elizabeth, I hardly expected an attractive woman of twenty-six to have had no previous relationships. And as the affair was over five years ago—'

'It was more than an affair,' she broke in desperately. 'We were married.'

'Married!' He looked thunderstruck. 'But when I proposed to you you never said a word.'

'I know I should have told you then,' she admitted miserably, 'but I wanted to leave the past behind, and I thought the marriage had been annulled.'

'Annulled?' He picked it up immediately. 'Then it wasn't a—'

'It was legal,' she said quickly, 'but it had never been... It wasn't a real marriage.'

'You said you *thought* it had been annulled?'

'I'd signed the papers, but Quinn hadn't.'

'So you're still legally married?'

'Yes. I'm sorry, I didn't mean to deceive you.'

'I'll contact my lawyers first thing in the morning. As the marriage hadn't been consummated, getting a speedy annulment shouldn't be a problem.'

Quinn, who had been standing silently by, spoke for the first time. 'I'm afraid that from your point of view there's one major problem.'

'What's that?' Richard demanded curtly.

'The marriage *hadn't* been consummated, but now...' He had no need to complete the sentence. His meaning was only too clear.

Richard, his fair face going brick-red, turned on Elizabeth. 'So after pretending not to know each other you two jumped into bed the instant my back was turned! Of all the lying, deceitful little bitches! You've made a complete fool of me...'

'I'm sorry; truly I am. I never meant to hurt you—'

As if she hadn't spoken, he stormed on, 'If you're expecting me to forgive you and go on with—'

'Wait a minute,' Quinn broke in firmly. 'Now Jo has said her piece and apologized, as *I* am the one who's largely responsible for all this, you can address the rest of your remarks to me.'

Dropping the ignition key into Elizabeth's hand, he opened the door and pushed her through. 'I won't be long. Wait for me in the car.'

The study door closed behind her with a decisive click. As she crossed the hall, she heard Richard's voice raised in fury. 'Damn you, Durville, if you think for one minute...'

When she reached the front door, as if by magic, the maid appeared to open it for her.

'Thank you, Mary... When Lady Beaumont gets back, will you please tell her I'm sorry to have to leave without giving proper notice?'

Though she looked surprised, the girl answered sedately, 'Certainly, Miss Cavendish.'

All of a tremble, Elizabeth crossed the pavement to where the Mercedes was parked and got in. But after a minute or so, feeling too restless to just sit and wait, she left the key in the ignition and went to walk in Lombard Square's tree-lined garden.

It was deserted except for an elderly man, muffled in a tweed overcoat and a scarf, who sat on a bench reading *The Times*, while almost at his feet a squirrel foraged amongst the fallen leaves.

Elizabeth followed the perimeter path, her thoughts agitated. She couldn't blame Richard for being furious; she'd let him down badly.

The only thing to be remotely thankful for was that he hadn't told his mother about their 'engagement'. If Lady Beaumont and his friends had known it would have made matters a great deal worse...

Completing the circuit, she was about to go around for

a second time when she noticed Quinn was by the car. Something about his attitude riveted her attention. He was standing absolutely still, his dark head bent, staring into space.

As she approached, he glanced up. His face held such desolation that she caught her breath. An instant later it was gone, making her wonder if she'd only imagined that look of bleak unhappiness.

But she knew she hadn't. So what had caused it?

Opening the car door for her, he said, 'I was just wondering where you'd got to.' His voice wasn't quite even.

That was it. When he'd come back to find the Mercedes empty and the key in the ignition, he must have presumed she'd gone.

Climbing in, she explained, 'I've just been taking a walk round the garden. I felt too restless to sit still.'

When he slid in beside her and started the engine, she asked, 'How...how did it go? I mean, was Richard very hurt...?'

'He was more angry than hurt,' Quinn said flatly. 'And it soon became obvious that a lot of his anger was caused by the fact that I'd deprived him of the Van Hamel, a diamond he particularly wanted.

'When I said I was quite prepared to let him have it, he pointed out that if I hadn't forced up the price in the first place it would have been his for four hundred thousand pounds.

'I argued for a while—for the look of the thing—before agreeing to let him have it for what he would have paid if I hadn't been there. He seemed to regard that as some kind of victory, so honour was satisfied...'

They drove for a while without speaking, then she asked, 'Where are we heading for now? Earlier you said you had some business to attend to.'

'I have. It's my intention to drop you at the cottage first.'

He sounded distracted, as though his thoughts were else-where, and she relapsed into silence.

By the time they reached Hawks Lane a blue-grey dusk was turning into early evening. Several of the cottage windows were lit, and the old-fashioned street lamps were casting pools of light.

With his usual courtesy, Quinn helped her out, lifted her case from the boot, and waited while she opened the door.

When he showed no sign of coming in, she said, 'Won't you have a sandwich and some coffee first? You didn't have any lunch.'

He shook his head. 'I'll get straight off.'

'What time will you be back? I'll have dinner ready.'

'I really can't say. But there's no need to bother with a meal for me.'

'It's no bother,' she said quickly.

He shook his head again. 'I can get something out. If I look like being very late I'll probably stay over at a hotel rather than disturb you.'

Suddenly fearful, she asked, 'Quinn, what's wrong?'

His expression sardonic, he asked, 'What could be wrong?'

He was stonewalling, and she knew it.

Was he still expecting her to run? He was certainly giving her every chance to. But, remembering that look of bleak unhappiness on his face when he'd thought she had gone, she took heart.

Handing him the key, she said, 'If you're very late you can let yourself in, so there'll be no need to disturb me. Though I shall probably wait up for you anyway.'

His smile was a shade wry, he dropped the key into his pocket and turned to go.

'Aren't you forgetting something?'

He glanced at her, one dark brow raised enquiringly.

Pursing her lips, she raised her face for his kiss. His

expression softened and, a smile tugging at the corners of his long mouth, he kissed her lightly.

Standing in the doorway, she watched him drive fifty yards or so, and turn the car. When he drew level once more, she blew him a kiss. In return he sketched an ironic salute.

With a sigh she went inside and closed the door behind her. Though she had finally decided that being with him was what really mattered, it seemed there was still a long way to go before their relationship stood any kind of chance.

All they had achieved so far was a kind of precarious balance. She had no idea what went on in his head. He didn't trust her an inch.

With time to kill, and unable to settle, she made up her mind to clean the cottage thoroughly. That way, if he decided to stick to the plan he'd outlined the previous day, she would be ready to leave for the States when he was.

By seven-thirty she had the whole place in order. The table, complete with fancy napkins and gold candles, was set, a bottle of white wine was cooling in the fridge, the starter was waiting to be served, and a chicken and vegetable casserole was bubbling away in the oven.

After checking that there was nothing left to do, she took a shower, then, dried and perfumed, brushed her long hair until it gleamed like black silk.

Having donned a red satin housecoat that had been a Christmas gift from Mrs Henderson—and deemed too glamorous for ordinary use—she dimmed the lights and settled down in front of the fire to wait.

At eight-thirty, her heart like lead, she turned the oven off. It might be hours before Quinn was back. If he returned at all. He'd said business... But what kind of business would take so long, and possibly necessitate staying overnight?

Too dispirited to eat a full-scale meal alone, she was about to make herself a sandwich when she heard a car draw up outside and a door slam.

As she held her breath, a key turned in the lock and Quinn came in, carrying a bunch of hothouse roses and his grip.

She went to meet him eagerly, gladly. This time when she lifted her face and he kissed her she put her arms round his neck and returned his kiss, her lips parting invitingly.

Just for an instant she felt him hesitate, and with an instinct as old as Eve deliberately leaned against him, her slender body pressed to his.

He dropped the things he was carrying, and with a sound almost like a groan took her in his arms and kissed her with a thoroughness that left her breathless and tingling.

'Mmm...' she murmured, revelling in a closeness that seemed to exceed the merely physical. 'That's more like it.'

Running his hand over her satin-covered curves, his voice shaken between passion and laughter, he said, 'You witch.'

'I hope you haven't eaten?' She made an effort to be practical. 'Dinner's all ready.'

His lips travelling down the side of her neck and finding the warm, silky skin of a shoulder, he muttered, 'Who cares about food?'

'I do,' she said firmly. 'I've gone to a lot of trouble over this meal.'

Releasing her reluctantly, he handed her the flowers, and picked up his grip. 'Give me a few minutes to shower and change.'

He returned quite quickly, freshly shaved, his dark hair still damp from the shower, and wearing a silk open-necked shirt and casual trousers.

Glancing at the candles, the centrepiece of red roses, and

the long-stemmed wine glasses, he remarked ironically, 'Very honeymoonish.'

Elizabeth produced and served the smoked salmon and prawn starter, while Quinn opened and poured the Chablis.

Raising her glass, she said, 'Here's to us.'

Looking at her over the rim of his own glass, his green eyes brilliant in the candlelight, he echoed, 'To us.' But his face was impassive, and she could sense a kind of wariness, a holding back.

Sighing inwardly, she faced the fact that though he'd only been upstairs a short time the previous closeness was gone, and a feeling of constraint had taken its place.

While they ate, she tried to think of something interesting to talk about, but her mind remained stubbornly blank.

After she had carried in and dished up the colourful casserole, determined to break the silence, she remarked, 'When it turned eight o'clock I began to wonder where you'd got to.'

'I had warned you I might be late,' he said evenly.

Aware, even as she spoke, that she sounded resentful, accusing, she said, 'You'd warned me you might not be back at all. But I couldn't see what kind of business would keep you out all night when—' She broke off.

'When it's our *honeymoon*?' he finished ironically.

Flushing a little, she reminded him, 'It was you who first mentioned the word.'

'That was before you ran away for the second time.'

So it was still foremost in his mind, still bothering him.

Firmly, she said, 'Well, I'm here now, and you won't find it easy to get rid of me.'

'You're starting to sound just like a wife.'

Rattled by the open mockery, she retorted, 'I *am* a wife.'

'However temporary?'

'You were the one who suggested that we stayed together until the fever had run its course.'

'Would you prefer it if I insisted on a lifetime commitment? Somehow I doubt it.'

Suddenly defeated, she bit her lip hard. This wasn't how she'd wanted it to be. Lifting her chin, she met his caustic gaze, and, her grey eyes filling with tears, despite all her efforts, said huskily, 'I'd prefer it if we didn't quarrel.'

His face softening, he apologized. 'I'm sorry. You've tried to make the evening special, and I'm being an absolute swine to you.' Reaching across the table, he took her hand, and lifting it to his lips, kissed her palm. 'Forgive me?'

Trying not to blink, she managed a tremulous smile. 'There's nothing to forgive.'

'Generous woman. But you may not feel so charitable when I tell you where I went after I'd left you.'

'Where did you go?' she asked curiously.

He refilled their wine glasses, before answering, 'To your old college, to see Peter Carradine.'

'I don't mind in the slightest,' she assured him. Then she said anxiously, 'I hope he's still there?'

'Yes. He's now head of the history department. When I explained who I was, he said how sorry he'd been to hear of my father's death. I asked if he recalled an ex-student of his going to work for Henry. He said, "Yes, Jo Merrill. I remember it well." But your story and his don't quite tally.'

'But they *must* do!' she cried. 'It was the truth.'

'It's certainly true that Henry went to him when he was looking for a secretary-cum-historian. However, it *isn't* true that Carradine mentioned your name to him.'

White to the lips, she cried, 'But that's what he told me.'

'He agrees he *told* you that, but it wasn't what really happened.'

'I don't understand,' she said weakly.

'It seems that Henry had been making his own enquiries and already knew about you. He asked Carradine to get in touch with you, say that *he* had recommended you, and virtually offer you the post.

'When Carradine asked why he didn't approach you directly, Henry said he considered that you were more likely to take the job if the offer came via a tutor you knew and respected.

'Carradine admitted that he'd felt uneasy about even such a mild deception, and said if he hadn't known Henry so well he would have thought twice about it.

'He wanted to know how things had turned out. I set his mind at rest by telling him that you and Henry had got along extremely well.

'It seems he'd thought very highly of you. He said that, despite a rather grim home life, you had been a sunny-natured girl. A girl who had had sense and courage and a rare honesty. Then he went on to ask if I knew what had become of you. When I told him you were my wife, he shook my hand and told me I was a lucky man.'

Elizabeth's hands, which had been clenched into fists, relaxed. 'So at least you know I wasn't lying about what happened.'

'What I *don't* know, and what puzzles me, is what Henry was up to. I don't believe for one minute the excuse he fed Carradine.'

Feeling almost light-headed with relief, she queried, 'After all this time, does it matter?'

Shrugging, he answered, 'Probably not.' But somehow his expression belied his words.

Unable to worry about what she saw as unimportant, Elizabeth removed the remains of the casserole, and brought in the apricot fool.

His lean, attractive face preoccupied, a little frown drawing his black brows together as though he was deep in thought, Quinn ate in silence.

When their bowls were empty, she pushed back her chair and rose.

Coming out of his brown study, he offered, 'I'll clear away and get the coffee. You sit in front of the fire and relax.'

Obediently she moved to the settee, and watched him deftly gather together the dishes, before disappearing kitchenwards.

It was warm and comfortable and, staring into the flames, she was soon blinking, drowsy as a cat.

By the time he returned with a tray of coffee and took a seat by her side, in spite of her late morning she was having to stifle her yawns.

Handing her a cup, he said, 'I haven't yet thanked you for a delicious dinner.' Quizzically, he added, 'I didn't know I'd married a woman who could cook.'

'At one time I couldn't. I took a cookery course when I got tired of eating microwave meals for one.'

Soberly, he observed, 'If you really were alone all those years it couldn't have been much fun.'

'I was, and it wasn't. Though one can get used to being alone.'

'What about your parents? Didn't you keep in touch with them? I gather from what Carradine said that they were somewhat strict and narrow-minded, but surely they would have provided some support?'

'They'd always done their best for me, but we'd never been very close. In any case, by that time they were both dead.

'When did they die? Before or after you'd started to work for Henry?'

'After. In fact just a week or so before my twenty-first birthday.'

'How did they die?'

'In an accident. My mother was accompanying my father—who'd had another heart attack—to hospital, when the emergency ambulance they were travelling in went off the road and rolled down an embankment. I learnt later that it had had a front tyre blow when they were doing a very high speed.'

Quinn grimaced. 'So you really were all alone.' Then he said violently, 'Damn Piery!'

Startled, she objected, 'It's hardly Piery's fault. He only did what he thought was right.'

'Don't imagine he was being altruistic. He did what he did for totally selfish reasons.'

'How can you say that, when he was so kind?'

'Did you ever ask yourself *why* he was being so kind?'

'I think he was concerned about me and—'

'Concerned be damned. He was responsible for the whole sorry mess.'

She felt moved to protest. 'How can you think such a thing?'

'I don't just *think*, I *know*.'

Helplessly, she said, 'But all he did was—'

'I don't just mean showing you my letter. It was Piery who started the ball rolling; he set out to cause trouble, and quite deliberately.'

As she began to shake her head, Quinn said flatly, 'Earlier this evening, he admitted as much.'

Her sleepiness fled. 'Then you've talked to him?'

'After I'd left Carradine I went to see him. I made it clear that I wanted the truth, and I was prepared to beat it out of him if necessary. I felt like breaking his neck anyway.'

'But why? I don't understand.'

'Haven't you ever wondered what brought me over to England in the first place?'

Light beginning to dawn, she breathed, 'You mean Piery…?'

'Exactly. It was Piery who first wrote and warned me that ''some pretty little nobody of a secretary'' was trying to get her hooks into Dad...

'I was extremely busy at the time and I didn't pay too much attention. Then he wrote again sounding really panicky, telling me about you visiting Henry's room late at night, and taking both money and gifts—'

'That's a lie!' she burst out furiously.

As if she hadn't spoken, Quinn went on, 'He said that Henry had fallen for you hook, line and sinker, and that when he'd tried to ''talk some sense'' into the old man he'd been sent off with a flea in his ear. He added that if I didn't do something quickly we'd end up with a twenty-one-year-old stepmother...'

'And you believed everything he told you!' she cried hoarsely.

'Enough to be concerned,' Quinn admitted. 'That was when I took a few days off and I came over to see for myself how things stood.

'It was immediately clear that Piery was right—there was a great deal more between you and Henry than any normal secretary-boss relationship.

'I watched you together. I saw the way you smiled at him and put your hand on his shoulder. I saw how his face lit up when you came into the room, and how he seldom took his eyes off you...

'But the bank was under threat from a hostile takeover bid and I was forced to return to Boston for a while. That was when I wrote to Piery.

'I came back to Saltmarsh as soon as I thought the bid had been defeated, and my earlier conviction—that Henry was besotted and you were leading him on—was, if anything, intensified...'

'I can see what it must have *looked* like,' she said helplessly, 'especially when you were expecting the worst. But you have to believe there was nothing other than fondness on either side.'

Quinn's shoulders moved in a slight shrug. 'Whether or not that's the truth, Piery seemed to genuinely believe that Henry was in love with you, and he was desperate to break things up. He didn't want you for a stepmother.'

'You mean he was afraid I'd get Henry's money?'

'That's what I always thought,' Quinn admitted, 'but there was a lot more to it than that.

'When I found you knew why I'd married you, I presumed that Henry must have learnt the truth from Piery and told you out of jealousy. But once I discovered it was Piery himself who had "blown the gaff", so to speak, it didn't make sense.

'You see, if the money, or saving Henry, had been his only concern, once you were married to me you would no longer have posed a threat.

'He knew I was under no illusions about what kind of woman you were, and well able to take care of myself, so why had it been necessary to show you my letter and encourage you to leave me?

'When you told me exactly what had happened, I knew there could only be one reason. And tonight he admitted it…'

Her eyes fixed on Quinn's dark face, she waited.

'Can't you guess?'

She shook her head.

'He was head over heels in love with you… You'd left Henry, and he wanted you to leave me. He was hoping you'd fall into his arms…'

Once it was put into words, she felt instinctively that Quinn was right. It explained both Piery's attitude and her own faint, inexplicable sense of unease…

'He'd been mad about you from the start, and when you virtually ignored him and showed every sign of preferring

Henry it made him as jealous as hell. He was desperate to stop Henry from marrying you; that's why he involved me. Though he hadn't visualized the results...

'And of course he paid for his interference in more ways than one. When you disappeared, and Henry discovered what had been going on, the balloon went up and he threw him out.'

So it had all been Piery's doing, Elizabeth thought dazedly. He'd turned all their lives upside down without a single qualm...

As though reading her mind and disagreeing, Quinn went on, 'Your disappearance, and the effect it had on everybody, shook Piery. He admitted that later, when he'd got over you, he was sorry for what he'd done.

'He realized our relationship had mattered a lot more than he'd first thought. That was why he tried to make amends by sending me that photograph of you and Beaumont...'

'If only he hadn't meddled in the first place,' she said sadly.

'I have to say that Piery wasn't wholly to blame. If there'd been no real truth in his tales, I would have dismissed them out of hand—'

'But there *wasn't*!' she broke in urgently. 'Everything he told you was either distorted or outright lies. I wish you'd believe that Henry and I were *fond* of each other, nothing more or less.'

'He left you half his fortune,' Quinn reminded her ruthlessly.

'I don't know why. I didn't want him to. And I certainly never took either money or gifts from him.'

'Tonight, when I pressed him, Piery confessed he'd made that part of it up to get me to come.'

'But you believed every word,' she pointed out indignantly. 'That's why you thought Henry had given me the earrings.'

'Are you still saying he didn't?'

'That's exactly what I'm saying.'

Sounding as if he was holding on to his patience with an effort, Quinn said, 'It no longer *matters*, so why don't you tell me the truth?'

'That *is* the truth.' With a gesture that showed her frustration, she went on, 'I know they're special, and, as you said, not the kind of thing one could buy from a market stall, but I can't understand why, now you know Piery lied, you should still be convinced they came from Henry.'

He sighed. 'Look, even if Piery had never suggested such a thing, I *know* Henry must have given them to you.'

'Well, you know wrong. He didn't.'

'Not even as a one-off present?'

She jumped to her feet. 'Not even as a one-off present!' Bitterly, she added, 'Nor did I take them.' That he could suspect her of being a thief still rankled.

'Listen to me,' he said evenly. 'I don't *care* if you took them. They're beautiful; I wouldn't blame you if you had been tempted—'

'How *kind* of you.'

'I just want you to admit—'

'There's nothing to admit. I *wasn't* tempted, and I *didn't* take them.'

One look at his face told her she was wasting her time. Going down on her knees by his side, she put a hand on his knee and, in a last desperate appeal, begged, 'Oh, Quinn, *please* believe me.'

'I *want* to believe you.' In a tortured voice he added, 'But there's just no way I can.'

Head bent, feeling helpless and defeated, she knelt like some supplicant who had been denied.

Almost roughly, he said, 'There's no need to look quite

so—' Breaking off abruptly, he got up and, putting his hands on her shoulders, urged her to her feet. 'Come on, you look all in; it's time you were in bed. I don't think you've fully recovered from the stress of yesterday.'

His arm around her waist, as though he feared she might collapse, he began to lead her towards the stairs. 'Before you get settled, I'd better fetch those pillows and blankets.'

'Pillows and blankets?' She glanced up at him. 'Whatever for?'

'I presumed you'd want me to sleep on the couch.'

All she wanted was for him to believe her. But if she couldn't move him she'd just have to live with it. She'd chosen the course she wanted to take, and there was no way she was going to give up now, or allow pride to come between them.

'No,' she answered levelly, 'I don't want you to sleep on the couch.'

CHAPTER TEN

ELIZABETH stirred and opened her eyes. It was still barely light, but a sparrow was chirping with cheerful persistence, and a moment later a blackbird began his morning hymn of praise.

She was stretched on her back, the weight of Quinn's arm lying just beneath her breasts, his year-round tan dark against her creamy skin.

Her decision not to let pride come between them had brought its own reward, and from a mind still sluggish and drugged with sleep came the remembrance of his lovemaking and the joy it had brought.

Moving her head cautiously, she contemplated her sleeping husband. He was lying on his side, his face turned towards her.

The bone structure was strong, and the face an undeniably tough one. But with the ironic eyes closed, and the confident mouth relaxed, his rumpled hair and the sweep of dark lashes gave him a look of vulnerability.

A look that filled her with a poignant love, and a longing for what might have been. As she continued to stare at him, as though the sheer intensity of her feelings had disturbed his sleep, he opened his eyes.

Her face full of unconscious warmth and tenderness, she smiled at him. Just for an instant his eyes held the look she'd always wanted to see in them, then they became veiled, as though he'd remembered things he would rather not have remembered.

Shaken, she fell back on practicalities, and, her voice as

steady as she could make it, asked, 'What are your plans for the day?'

He pushed himself up on one elbow before answering, 'I still have Henry's safe and some notebooks to look through, so after breakfast I propose to go back to Saltmarsh.'

'You said *I*. Does that mean you intend to go alone?'

'It means there's no need for you to come if you would prefer not to. You can always stay here.'

'I'd rather come.'

'Very well.' It was impossible to tell whether he was pleased or sorry.

She asked the question that had been at the back of her mind. 'Have you decided what you're going to do about the house?'

'In what way?'

'You indicated you might be thinking of selling it.'

'And you don't want me to?'

'Henry wouldn't have wanted you to.'

'Then perhaps he should have left it to Piery.'

'I think he guessed Piery would sell it.' Carefully, she added, 'But I don't think he expected *you* to.'

'Are you trying to make me feel bad about it?'

About to say no, she changed it to, 'Yes.'

Wryly, he asked, 'Decided on absolute honesty?'

'Up to a point.'

Quinn's face lightened, and laughter-lines appeared at the corners of his eyes. 'Then tell me something: do you really dislike eating in bed?'

'That depends.'

'On what?'

'On whether I'm alone or not. What about you? Do you like eating in bed?'

'I can think of better things to do.'

'Such as?'

'Want me to show you?'

'Yes, please,' she said demurely. 'If we have time.'

He pretended to consider. 'Well, I don't care to rush these things, but no doubt with a little cooperation...'

Later they shared a shower—which, allowing for the enjoyment factor, took somewhat longer than usual—before dressing together.

When Elizabeth had brushed her hair and coiled it into its usual smooth chignon, she fastened Henry's silver locket around her neck.

Glancing up, she saw Quinn watching her, his eyes cold. So he was still jealous. Sighing, she went to scramble some eggs and make the coffee.

As they sat over the breakfast table and she watched him butter his toast, she thought sadly that even now they were together there were still doubts and mistrust, rather than the mental closeness she longed for...

Catching a fleeting glimpse of her expression, and misinterpreting it, Quinn asked, 'More regrets?'

'No.' Realizing he'd heard the slight hesitation, she added firmly, 'At least not in the way you mean.'

'Then in what way?'

'I was regretting what we might have had if...if things had been different.'

'You mean if you could bring yourself to tell me the truth about the earrings? Or I could bring myself to accept a lie?'

'No, that isn't what I mean. I wouldn't want you to accept a lie. But I would like you to believe the truth.'

'I no doubt will, when I hear it.'

She bit her lip until she tasted blood, the minor pain helping to eclipse the major. Then, knowing there was no way she could win, and determined not to get embroiled again, she said flatly, 'I'd rather not talk about it.'

'Why not, if you're really on the side of the angels?'

'I don't see the point, as I'm never going to be able to convince you that I'm speaking the truth…'

'If you didn't get them from Henry, why were you so unwilling to tell me where they did come from?'

Bristling, she jumped to her feet. 'I didn't see why I should *have* to tell you. I wanted you to trust me.'

'I wish I could.'

Agitation making her clumsy, she gathered together some of the breakfast dishes and, cutlery rattling, went through to the kitchen.

Picking up the rest, he followed her.

Putting the dishes in the sink with unnecessary violence, she ran the hot water, squirted in some bubbles, and began to wash them.

Instead of going away, he picked up a cloth and began to dry them with maddening efficiency.

Without in the least meaning to, she burst out angrily, 'I just can't understand why you're so *sure* the earrings came from Henry.'

'Believe me, I have a very good reason.'

'Then tell me what it is.'

He shook his head. 'First I want to hear your version of where they came from.'

Seeing her expression grow obstinate, he said trenchantly, 'The time for playing games is over, Jo. I want to know *how* you came by them, and I want to know *now*.'

She hesitated, while the desire to tell him the truth and a certain inbuilt reluctance to be browbeaten battled it out.

Finally, she said, 'Very well, I'll tell you. My natural mother left them to me—'

'Your *natural* mother?'

'It's a long story.'

'I think you'd better come and sit down.'

She dried her hands, and, returning to the living room,

sat down on the settee, while Quinn leaned a shoulder against the fireplace and waited.

Having collected her thoughts, she began, 'I didn't know I'd been adopted until after both my parents, or at least the people I'd always looked on as my parents, were killed.

'It was then I discovered that my real mother had died from some infection when I was only a few days old, and the woman I'd always looked on as my mother was actually my aunt. I was the child of her younger sister.'

'What became of your natural father?'

'I've no idea. I understand my mother wasn't married, and when she died no one came forward.'

'So your aunt and uncle stepped in?'

'Yes. When my mother became ill they agreed that it was their duty to take care of me if anything happened to her...'

'What about the earrings?'

'She'd left them for me as a twenty-first-birthday present, along with a letter that said they were her most precious possession—'

'You told me you didn't have them when I first knew you,' Quinn objected sharply.

'I didn't. In fact at that time I didn't even know of their existence.'

'Go on,' he ordered.

'It seems they'd been lodged with my aunt's solicitors, and by the time they tried to contact me my aunt and uncle were dead and the flat was empty.

'It was after I'd left you... I was looking for job opportunities in one of the papers when I happened to catch sight of an advertisement. It said something along the lines of, "If Miss Josian Elizabeth Merrill will get in touch with Firkin and Jones solicitors, she may well learn something to her advantage."

'At first I was afraid to answer it...' Watching Quinn's

lips thin, she added, 'It was only a short time since I'd managed to give your detective the slip, and I thought it might be a trap.

'But just then I was desperately short of money, and finding it a struggle to pay the rent for my bedsit, so finally I was forced to risk it...'

'If you were hoping for some financial help you must have been terribly disappointed?'

She shook her head. 'No, I wasn't disappointed.'

'The earrings must be worth quite a lot,' he pointed out brusquely. 'If you were so desperate why didn't you sell them?'

'I wouldn't have dreamt of selling them,' she informed him coldly. 'I was thrilled to bits when I realized that they'd belonged to my real mother.'

'Even though you'd never known her?'

'Maybe for that very reason.'

They had been something concrete from the past, a priceless gift to keep and cherish. When she'd read the accompanying letter she felt sad, yet, in an odd way, close to the unknown woman who'd given birth to her.

'It seems my aunt and uncle had intended to tell me that I'd been adopted when I reached twenty-one. But of course fate stepped in, and I learnt it from papers they'd kept.

'At first I felt bitter that they hadn't told me earlier. I could have asked about my real mother, known what kind of person she was, what she looked like, if I resembled her at all...'

Elizabeth sighed. 'But of course it was far too late. All I had was one short, shakily written letter and the earrings.'

Quinn was watching her, his green eyes guarded. 'And that's your story? You don't want to change it?'

'Why should I want to change it?' she asked angrily. 'It's the truth... You don't suspect me of making it all up? If I was that clever I'd be writing fiction!'

'Isn't that what this is?'

She felt a terrible sense of despair. Piery had done far more harm than he'd ever imagined.

Lifting her chin, she suggested quietly, 'Surely there should be some way of checking with the solicitors?'

'Probably. If they're still in business?'

'I don't know if they are,' she said uncertainly. 'They were only a small, back-street firm, and it was almost five years ago.'

'Where were their offices?'

'In Whitechapel.'

His voice holding more than a hint of challenge, he suggested, 'Would you like to go over and see if they're still there?'

She hesitated. Suppose they weren't? But if they weren't, apart from raising her hopes for nothing, she would be no worse off.

'Yes, I would,' she said firmly.

But, noting her hesitation, his face cynical, Quinn observed, 'You don't appear very sanguine.'

Gritting her teeth, she retorted, 'Oh, but I am.'

'Then we'll pay them a visit before we start for Saltmarsh.'

Some ten minutes later they left Cantle Cottage and headed east through London's traffic. The day was cold and bright. A stiffish breeze battered signs and awnings and sent puffs of grey cloud scurrying across the sky like smoke signals.

They were approaching Whitechapel before Quinn broke the silence to ask, 'You do know the address?'

'I don't recall the name of the street,' Elizabeth admitted, 'but it's off Rockwell Road. There used to be a big, old-fashioned pub on the corner. It was painted blue.'

Halfway down Rockwell Road, Quinn said suddenly, 'This looks like it. Cranton Street.'

'That's right,' she said eagerly. 'It comes back to me now. It's a cul-de-sac, and the offices were at the bottom end.'

They drove the length of the street, and Elizabeth's heart sank. There was a garishly painted mini-market where she'd hoped to see the funereal-looking window she remembered from five years previously. So it had turned out to be a wild-goose chase after all...

'That looks like it.' Quinn's voice, sounding strange, broke into her gloomy thoughts. She followed the direction of his gaze and realized she'd been looking on the wrong side of the road.

Pulling over, he parked the car on the uneven frontage, where the wind had rounded up and corralled a small pile of litter, and helped her out.

The black and gold writing on the glass proclaiming 'Firkin and Jones Solicitors' was peeling a little, and the whole place had an air of once prosperous respectability gone slightly to seed.

Inside the black-painted door, the carpet and the decor had a faded elegance that harked back to palmier days.

A neatly dressed, middle-aged woman looked up from behind an old-fashioned desk in the corner. 'Good morning. Can I help you?'

Elizabeth found her voice. 'My husband and I were hoping to make some enquiries with regard to a small legacy I received about five years ago. It had been lodged here, pending my twenty-first birthday, by a Mr and Mrs Christopher Merrill, my adoptive parents, on behalf of my natural mother.'

'And your name at the time?'

'Josian Elizabeth Merrill. I came in answer to your advertisement.'

'Can you tell me which partner handled the matter?'

'Mr Jones.'

'I'll see if he's free. If you'd like to take a seat for a moment...?'

Elizabeth complied, while Quinn remained standing, his hands thrust negligently into his jacket pockets, his broad shoulders against the panelling.

Elizabeth glanced at him. Though his posture was relaxed, and his face gave nothing away, she could sense a hidden core of tension.

The receptionist, who had disappeared into some inner sanctum, returned after several minutes, to advise them that, 'Mr Jones will see you, if you'd like to come this way.'

They followed her into a stuffy, overheated office where a small, dapper man with a skull-like face, shrewd blue eyes and impossibly black hair rose to greet them.

Yes, she recognized him, Elizabeth thought, her heart beating faster. But common sense insisted that he was hardly likely to remember her.

'Do sit down.' He waved them to a pair of red leather chairs that had once been handsome but were now frankly worn and, resuming his own seat, asked, 'Now, how can I help you?'

Elizabeth repeated what she'd told the receptionist.

The solicitor opened a file that lay ready on his desk and consulted it for a moment, before querying, 'Your birthday is September the seventeenth, and your natural mother's name was Elizabeth Smith?'

'That's right,' she said eagerly.

'So what exactly do you wish to know?'

Before she could speak, Quinn asked in the voice of a stranger, 'Can you tell me what form this legacy took?'

'The description here merely states a pair of antique earrings.' Looking up, Mr Jones went on, 'But if my memory serves me correctly they were *most* unusual. The early seventeenth-century craftsmanship, something I've always been interested in, was quite superb.'

Pulling his wallet from his pocket, Quinn shook the earrings into his palm and held them out for the other man's inspection.

'Anything like those?'

The sharp blue eyes studied them. 'Exactly like those.'

'Thank you.' Quinn returned the earrings to his wallet and rose to his feet. 'We need take up no more of your time.'

A hand beneath her elbow, he urged a somewhat dazed Elizabeth to her feet. At the door she turned to add her own, belated thanks.

When they were back in the car, Quinn turned to her and said shortly, 'It seems I owe you an apology.'

She shook her head. 'I don't want an apology. I'm just happy that you know the truth.'

But even as she spoke she was shaken to realize that *he* was far from happy. His face was set and serious, as though the truth had come as a most unpleasant shock to him.

Chilled and disconcerted, she lapsed into silence.

The first half of the journey proved to be far from comfortable. What little conversation there was sounded forced and stilted, and Quinn avoided even glancing in her direction.

As the afternoon wore on, they stopped for coffee and sandwiches at a country pub, but neither finished them.

The second half of the journey was, if anything, worse. Quinn's face looked even more bleak and sombre, and Elizabeth's spirits had sunk to rock-bottom.

When they reached the coast, the tide was out and they were able to drive straight over the causeway. Elizabeth was so upset and despondent that she hardly gave the previous traumatic crossing a thought.

Once inside the house, like a man driven by God knew what anxieties, Quinn headed straight for the study.

Hanging up her coat, she followed, to find he had already

opened Henry's wall safe and was taking things from it and stacking them on the desk.

His face was set and there was a curious urgency about his movements. He gave the impression of being braced for some impending calamity.

The air struck cold, and knowing how considerate he usually was of her comfort, she wondered why he hadn't stopped to light the fire.

Seriously perturbed, convinced now that something was dreadfully wrong, she raked through the ashes, put a match to a little pile of kindling, and, having blown it into life, made a wigwam of sticks.

When it was flaming cheerfully, she piled on some split logs, and, her heart heavy with fear, sat huddled by the blaze, her eyes on Quinn.

He had almost emptied the safe when he came to a small oblong case. Using his thumbnail, he pressed the catch and lifted the lid.

For what seemed an age, he stood motionless, staring at the contents. Then, with a look on his face that froze her to the marrow, he came over and handed her the case.

She found herself staring down at a brooch. Made of silver and mother-of-pearl, intricately curved into the shape of a mermaid, it was both old and beautiful. Her breath caught in her throat, she looked up at him wordlessly.

Taking the earrings from his wallet, he placed them alongside the brooch and, his voice curiously flat, said, 'A perfectly matched set. Though I'd only seen the brooch once before, and briefly, I knew I couldn't be mistaken.'

'So that was why you were so sure Henry had either given me the earrings or I'd taken them?'

'I didn't dare let myself believe anything else. Then, when the solicitor confirmed your story...'

He ran a hand over his eyes and, sounding like a man

on the rack, asked harshly, 'You understand what this means, don't you?'

Bemused, and having had no time to think, she shook her head.

'Do you remember me telling you about my childhood? About a girl named Beth who came to live with us...?'

As she struggled to make sense of what she was hearing, he went on heavily, 'You were right that Henry didn't keep a diary in the conventional sense. But the other day I discovered that, from being a young man, he had filled notebook after notebook with a daily account of everything that mattered to him.

'From one of those notebooks, I learned that Beth's full name was Elizabeth Smith. Henry called her the love of his life. He wanted her to marry him, but she refused. When he discovered she was having his baby, he begged her to change her mind.

'Maybe he pressured her too much, because one day, when he'd gone to London, she kissed me goodbye and walked out.

'She left a note telling Henry that she'd started to feel trapped. That she loved him, but she had to be a free spirit and couldn't bear to be tied down...

'He did his best to trace her, and, when he failed, tortured himself with the thought of her having an abortion...

'But if she'd had any such intention it seemed she changed her mind... The dates match exactly...'

As Elizabeth stared at him in dawning horror, he added, 'There's a strong probability that you're Henry's daughter.'

'B-but I *can't* be,' she stammered. 'That makes me...'

His face grey, he said, 'My half-sister.'

All at once there was blood pounding in her head. A blackness caught her up and threatened to envelop her... Somehow she fought it off. 'No! I don't believe I'm

Henry's daughter!' Yet everything pointed to it being the truth, and it made sense of so many things...

Heavily, Quinn said, 'Henry obviously thought you were. It explains his affection for you; why he left you half his estate; why he was so distraught when you vanished, and so furious with Piery and myself—'

'But it doesn't explain one very important thing,' she broke in urgently. 'He *knew* we were going to be married. I *told* him. If he as much as *suspected* that I was his daughter, why did he allow our wedding to go ahead? Why was he so *pleased* about it? And he was pleased—I'd stake my life on it.'

Quinn's head came up and the grey, beaten look gave way to a gleam of hope.

His voice holding a sharpening excitement, he suggested, 'Let's see if there's anything in those notebooks that will throw any light on it.'

Striding across to the desk, he unlocked the bottom drawer and began to take out the various piles of books. 'They're all dated and in order, thank the Lord, so we can soon find any that could be relevant.'

Even as he spoke he was looking through them, putting some aside, pushing the others away.

Bringing a little stack back to the fireside, he offered Elizabeth a thick, spiral-bound book with a blue cover. 'This is one of the earlier ones, where he talks about Beth. I thought you might like to see that. The others date from around six years ago.'

As though under compulsion, she took it and started to read, while he began to search through the later ones.

It was Quinn who first lifted his head and broke the silence. His voice strained, he said, 'Well, it's all here. But it doesn't make sense...

'Though he'd married again, it seems he'd never totally

given up hope of finding Beth and his child, and over the years had spent a small fortune trying to trace her.

'But with no idea where she'd head for he had very little to go on. She'd never mentioned anything about her background, or having a family, and Smith is a very common name.

'It seems his detectives followed endless false trails, and it wasn't until you were grown-up that they finally managed to get a lead, and began to piece together the facts of your birth and subsequent adoption.

'By the time you left college, Henry was fairly sure that he'd found his daughter. That's why he approached Peter Carradine and got him to offer you a job as his secretary. He wanted to get to know you, and be absolutely *certain* before he said anything... He asked you about your parents?'

'Yes.'

'And of course, with you believing that your aunt and uncle *were* your parents, your answer didn't help. After thinking it over, he decided to go and see them, and put his cards on the table.

'They admitted you were adopted, and told him who your natural mother was, but asked him not to say anything, as they wanted to tell you themselves when you reached twenty-one in a few weeks' time.

'But then their sudden deaths threw everything into chaos. He decided to wait until you'd got over the shock and things had returned to normal before telling you that he believed he was your father.

'It was shortly after that that I turned up and events began to move at top speed.

'Now comes the puzzling part. Henry wrote, and I quote:

'"Jo is a lovely-natured girl, the sort of daughter any man could be proud of. She has more than a look of Beth, and the same kind of radiance.

'"Quinn couldn't keep his eyes off her, and it was clear from the start that those two were in love. When Jo told me they were going to be married, I was absolutely delighted. I admit I don't understand the need for secrecy, but young people live by their own rules, and Quinn has always been something of an enigma.

'"When I heard the good news I was tempted to suggest to Jo that, as her father, I gave her away. But to have sprung it on her like that could have proved unsettling, and Quinn might well have objected to having his plans disrupted, so I've decided to wait until they return from honeymoon to tell them the truth."'

Quinn spread his hands in a gesture made up of despair and bafflement. 'Henry *must* have realized the implications, so what in God's name was he playing at? *Why* didn't he stop us marrying?'

Elizabeth took a deep breath, and, picking up the notebook she'd been reading, said, 'I've got another puzzle for you. I'll start at the beginning of the page. Listen to this.

'"Beth took the earrings I'd given her—perhaps she was wearing them—but either by design or accident she left the brooch... I'm trying to believe that this is a sign, that she'll change her mind and come back to me.

'"In the meantime I shall do all I can to trace her. If she won't come back, at least I'll be able to help, give her financial support. Please God, she won't destroy our child. *I've longed for a child of my own...*"'

She lifted wide grey eyes. 'But he had *you* then...'

Quinn, who had been sitting momentarily transfixed, leapt to his feet, and started to search through the other notebooks. When he found the one he wanted, he opened it and began to skim through it with undisguised eagerness.

Having paused to read a page, he said quietly, 'It seems my mother was five months pregnant when she met and married Henry. She and her young lover had been going to get married when he was killed in a motorcycling accident. Though Henry gave me his name, I'm not his son, thank God.'

Looking drained, as if even his magnificent strength and energy had been exhausted, Quinn came back to the hearth and dropped into his chair.

'What a sorry mix-up the whole thing's been, and I'm very largely to blame. If I hadn't been fool enough to believe everything Piery told me... If I'd watched you and Henry together with unbiased eyes—'

'There are so many ifs,' she said simply. 'If Henry had spoken out earlier. If my adoptive parents had told me the truth...'

Quinn looked up, his face sombre. 'The only one completely free from blame is you, and you're the one who's been made to suffer the most. I don't wonder you came to hate me—'

'I've *never* hated you.'

'You left me twice.'

'I've told you, it wasn't because I hated you.'

'Well, it certainly wasn't because you loved me,' he said sardonically.

'That's where you're wrong.' It was suddenly terribly important to convince him. 'This may be the only time I'll ever say this, but, whether you believe it or not, I *do* love you. I've always loved you. But one-sided loving can be humiliating and bitter... That's what made it so hard to stay with you.'

His voice level, devoid of emotion, he asked, 'Do you intend to stay with me now?'

'You said you wanted me…you wanted me to stay until the fever had died.'

'I've changed my mind. I don't want you. At least not on those terms.'

Suddenly icy cold, she asked, 'Then on what terms?'

'I want a lifetime's commitment. I want you to love me and stay with me for as long as we both shall live. Perhaps it's what I've always wanted, though for many reasons I haven't been able to say so. It seems utter madness to love a woman who—'

'Do you love me?' she broke in with sudden urgency.

'I've called what I feel for you a lot of things, but I guess love is the only word that will do in the end…

'But you haven't answered my question. Do you intend to stay with me?'

About to tease him a little, she saw the tenseness in his neck and shoulder muscles, the whiteness of his knuckles where his hand lay clenched on the chair-arm, and said simply, 'Yes.'

He swallowed hard. 'Then tomorrow we'll go and get you a ring.'

'There's no need. I already have one.' Unfastening Henry's round silver locket, she opened it, and tipped an exquisite chased white-gold wedding-ring into her palm.

'After I'd left you, I realized I was still wearing it. I wanted to send it back, but somehow, though it was like rubbing salt into a wound, I couldn't bear to part with it.'

His voice constricted, he said, 'So you kept it? I imagined you must have sold it years ago.'

Holding it out, she asked, 'Perhaps you'll put it on for me?'

Going down on his knees, he slid it on to her third finger and lifted her hand to his lips.

'My heart's darling.' His voice was unsteady.

Putting her arms around him, she cradled his dark head to her breast. 'Do you remember what you once called me?'

'My pleasure, my passion, my pain... You've been all of those.'

'And you mine.'

'Well, from now on we can leave the third emotion out. We've had enough pain. As for pleasure and passion—' lifting his head, he kissed her deeply '—we've the rest of our lives to enjoy those.'

'Starting now?' she asked hopefully.

'Starting now.'

The fire was glowing red. Stripping off her clothes, he laid her down in front of it, her dark head on a cushion, then, his own clothes joining the pile, stretched out beside her.

Pleasure and passion mingled sweetly, finally reaching the heights and exploding, incandescent as a shower of meteorites across a sky of black velvet.

For a while they lay quietly, saying nothing, merely touching. Lovers still.

It was Elizabeth who eventually broke the silence to ask tentatively, 'Quinn... You will forgive Piery?'

'Will you?'

'I already have. If he hadn't sent you that photograph, we wouldn't be here together now.'

'Well, if you look at it that way...'

'I'm too happy not to.'

She was rewarded with a kiss. Then, showing how close they were, Quinn asked, 'Something else on your mind?'

'I was wondering... Even if we live in the States, you'll keep Saltmarsh, won't you?'

'How could I deprive our children of their English heritage? We could even live here for part of the year, if you'd like to.'

She sighed. 'I hope Henry knows.'

Quinn's arms tightened around her and, his cheek against her hair, he said firmly, 'I'm sure he does.'

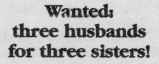

If you enjoyed what you just read,
then we've got an offer you can't resist!

Take 2 bestselling
love stories FREE!
Plus get a FREE surprise gift!

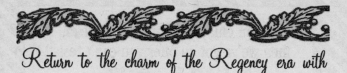

Return to the charm of the Regency era with

GEORGETTE
HEYER,

creator of the modern Regency genre.

Enjoy six romantic collector's editions with forewords
by some of today's bestselling romance authors,

**Nora Roberts, Mary Jo Putney,
Jo Beverley, Mary Balogh,
Theresa Medeiros and Kasey Michaels.**

Frederica
On sale February 2000

The Nonesuch
On sale March 2000

The Convenient Marriage
On sale April 2000

Cousin Kate
On sale May 2000

The Talisman Ring
On sale June 2000

The Corinthian
On sale July 2000

Available at your favorite retail outlet.

HARLEQUIN®
Makes any time special ™

Visit us at www.romance.net

PHGHGEN

Back by popular demand are

DEBBIE MACOMBER's

Hard Luck, Alaska, is a
town that needs women!
And the O'Halloran brothers
are just the fellows
to fly them in.

Starting in March 2000 this beloved series returns
in special 2-in-1 collector's editions:

MAIL-ORDER MARRIAGES, featuring
Brides for Brothers and *The Marriage Risk*
On sale March 2000

FAMILY MEN, featuring
Daddy's Little Helper and *Because of the Baby*
On sale July 2000

THE LAST TWO BACHELORS, featuring
Falling for Him and *Ending in Marriage*
On sale August 2000

Collect and enjoy each MIDNIGHT SONS story!

Available at your favorite retail outlet.

HARLEQUIN®
Makes any time special ™

Come escape with Harlequin's new

Series Sampler

Four great full-length Harlequin novels bound together in one fabulous volume and at an unbelievable price.

Be transported back in time with a Harlequin Historical® novel, get caught up in a mystery with Intrigue®, be tempted by a hot, sizzling romance with Harlequin Temptation®, or just enjoy a down-home all-American read with American Romance®.

You won't be able to put this collection down!

On sale February 2000 at your favorite retail outlet.

HARLEQUIN®
Makes any time special ™

Visit us at www.romance.net

PHESC

HARLEQUIN PRESENTS®

He's a ruthless businessman, an expert lover—
and he's 100% committed to staying single.

Until now. Because suddenly
he's responsible for a **BABY!**

HIS BABY

An exciting new miniseries
from Harlequin Presents®

*He's sexy, he's successful...
and now he's facing up to fatherhood!*

On sale February 2000:
Facing up to Fatherhood
by MIRANDA LEE
Harlequin Presents, #2087

On sale April 2000:
The Unexpected Wedding Gift
by CATHERINE SPENCER
Harlequin Presents, #2101

And look out for more later in 2000!

Available wherever Harlequin books are sold.

HARLEQUIN®
Makes any time special ™